BOYSTOWN 10: GIFTS GIVEN

MARSHALL THORNTON

D1707137

Kenmore Books

ISBN-13: 978-1979274821
ISBN-10: 1979274827
Edited by Joan Martinelli
Cover design by Marshall Thornton
Image by Stefanie Mohr 123RF Stock Photos
marshallthornton.wordpress.com

 Created with Vellum

Acknowledgments

I would like to thank Joan Martinelli, Randy and Valerie Trumbull, Kevin E. Davis, Kayla Jameth, William Miller, Ulysses Dietz and Ellen Sue Feinberg. Also a special thanks to the Chicago Tribune Archives.

Chapter One

GIVEN WHAT I'VE SEEN, given what I've lived, it strikes me that love is a kind of madness. An insanity that poses as a necessity, tricking us into believing we need it as much as breath, as much as life itself. A sensible man would run from it, bar the doors, hide in a cupboard like a child, rifle through the kitchen drawers looking for a weapon to stave it off. A sensible man would have nothing to do with love. I am not a sensible man.

A week before Christmas, a Tuesday, I asked my friend Brian to go shopping with me. I needed his help picking out a gift for my live-in boyfriend, Joseph Biernacki, which was how we ended up standing in a very long line, empty-handed, waiting to get into Marshall Field's Walnut Room for lunch. We'd done exactly forty-five minutes of shopping, most of it spent looking at watches even though I knew that was the wrong gift for Joseph. He'd given me a Swatch for our six-month anniversary, so a watch felt wrong, repetitive and unoriginal. Besides, I'd accidentally thrown the Swatch he'd given me away—and I didn't want to remind him. I was also a little afraid he'd buy me a new one for Christmas.

"You know, lunch is going to take two hours," I pointed out. "Maybe we should go out to State Street and buy a slice of pizza." There were greasy little pizza places roughly every two blocks.

"Isn't this a Chicago tradition, though? A Christmas lunch at Field's?" Brian asked. He'd grown up downstate. But he was right, lunch at Field's was a Christmas tradition. Hence the line we were in.

It was something I'd done a dozen times as a child. My mother, like thousands of mothers, had brought my brothers and me each year for shopping and lunch. Unfortunately, whatever fond memories I had of that had been obliterated by the fact that the last time I was in Field's I'd been shot at.

"It's not a tradition I need to repeat," I said.

He read the impatience on my face and said, "Hold on a second," before walking up to the hostess stand. After a brief conversation he turned and waved at me to join him.

When I got there, the hostess smiled and said, "Right this way."

As we walked through the atrium, passing the giant, three-story Christmas tree, I whispered into Brian's ear. "How did you manage this?"

"You'll see."

The hostess led us across the wood-paneled dining room —presumably walnut given the name of the place—to a table that sat in the corner in front of two enormous windows looking out at a random collection of Loop office buildings. Sugar Pilson sat alone at a table for four. She was casual but elegant in a cabled cream-colored sweater and a pair of washed-out, high-waisted jeans. Her hair was pulled back into a ponytail and she looked more like the cheerleader she was rumored to have once been than the socialite she actually was. I'd met her years before on a case, but she was now more Brian's friend than mine. Not that I didn't like her immensely, it's just that she and Brian did charity work together for Howard Brown, creating a bond between them I wasn't part of.

Obviously, Brian had known Sugar was there, so why had we waited in line at all? Were they planning to pretend we were meeting accidentally?

As soon as the hostess walked away, I said, "This is a setup, isn't it? What's going on?"

"Of course it's a set-up, darling. I need to have a professional conversation with you."

I took off my trench coat and threw it over the fourth chair beside Sugar's white fox car coat. Brian slipped his down jacket over the back of his chair.

"Why not just come to my office?" I asked as I sat down.

"I've driven by your office. Really Nick, how do you expect to attract clients? Your name isn't on the door and it looks like the kind of place you'd go for a back alley abortion."

She wasn't wrong. My office was hardly appealing.

"Abortion is legal, Sugar, and you're too young to know anything about back alley abortions."

"I'm not, but it's sweet of you to say so."

"So, what exactly do you need?"

She didn't answer, though, since a waitress showed up. "Can I get you something from the bar?"

"Yes, please. I'll have one of those wonderful coffee drinks you make," Sugar said, then she looked at Brian and me and said, "Perfect for a day like today."

Outside, it was in the low twenties and threatening to snow. Though in all honesty, I doubted Sugar had experienced much of the weather walking from her front door to the limo and from the limo into Field's. She'd probably been outside for a whole minute and a half.

"I'll have the same," I said.

"Can I have a diet Coke?" Brian asked.

When the waitress walked away, I asked Sugar again, "Why do you need my professional services?"

She took a moment, chewed some of the pink lipstick off her lower lip, and finally said, "I've fallen in love."

"And like most women the first thing you thought about was hiring a private detective?"

"Nick, don't tease her," Brian said. "It's not nice."

"Sorry. I assume you think this gentleman is after your money."

"Oh, I know he's after my money," Sugar said. "They always are. I need to know more about him so I can decide how much I want to spend on him."

"That's an interesting attitude," I said.

"Well, it's not like I can flip him over and check the price tag."

Brian giggled at the image.

"All right. What's his name?" I asked.

"There's one more thing."

"Okay."

"I have the feeling I'm being watched," Sugar said. "It's a feeling I don't like."

"Why do you feel that way?"

"Things keep showing up in Gloria's column. Things that shouldn't be there."

Gloria Silver wrote "The Silver Spoon" for the *Daily Herald*. We had a long, unpleasant association. She was the wife of the late Earl Silver, who originally wrote the column. He was also the lover of my friend (and onetime fuck buddy) Ross. I suppose that made us sexual relatives in a way. An extremely unpleasant thought.

I read her column every day, and Sugar was right, she'd been in the column a lot. Several of the mentions had to do with her drinking habits, the others weren't much more flattering.

"And do you think your new beau is the source of Gloria's information?"

"No, she's written about things he couldn't know."

"So you think Gloria's having you followed?"

"Oh God, that sounds so paranoid when you say it out loud."

The waitress brought our drinks. I took a spoon and stirred mine up. It was topped with whipped cream. Whipped cream and mustaches don't go well together in public. I took a sip; it was warm and sweet and very strong.

"You can help her, right Nick?" Brian asked.

I wasn't exactly ready to commit. "Tell me about the man."

"He's an artist. I met him at a gallery about two months ago. He paints orchids and flamingos on gigantic canvases. I bought a flamingo for my dining room. That's how we got to know each other."

"It's a great painting," Brian said.

"Isn't it?" Sugar said. "I think it just makes the room."

"How much was this great painting?"

"Hardly anything."

"Hardly anything in my world is twenty bucks," I pointed out. "How much is it in yours?"

"Five thousand."

"Are you his only client?"

"Goodness no. He sells all the time."

"He's very popular," Brian added.

"How long does it take him to paint a picture?"

"A couple of weeks. It's hard to tell. He works on more than one at a time."

"So he makes roughly ten grand a month and you think he might be after your money?"

"Darling, I clip coupons. And I never touch my principal." She also lived lavishly and gave generously, meaning that her income was large enough to impress people who made ten grand a month.

"You clip coupons? I hope that's just an expression. I don't like to think of you having a lot of bearer bonds lying around the house." Bearer bonds were not registered to their owner and therefore a very convenient thing to steal. They'd also gone out of fashion and, if I wasn't mistaken, weren't being issued anymore.

"Of course it's an expression," she said. "And I don't keep anything valuable around the house." Except the paintings on her walls, the furs in her closet and, I'd guess, a couple handfuls of diamonds lying about.

"We should get back on topic. We were talking about your painter. Michael France."

"Oh Nick, you know his name! You're psychic, aren't you? That must be so useful in your line of work."

"I read 'The Silver Spoon.' Gloria has been promoting him for a while now. A year? Longer?"

"How can you read that dreadful witch?" We'd both had run-ins with Gloria. It was something we had in common. Gloria hated both of us.

"I read her because I like to know what the witch is up to." Of course, it was obvious that Sugar read the column every day herself. Then something occurred to me. Michael France was a sort of protégé of Gloria's, or possibly...

"Sugar? Did you steal Gloria's boyfriend?"

"I wouldn't phrase it exactly like that."

Brian, though, was furiously nodding his head.

"Wait a minute," I said. "Didn't you tell me that Gloria was in love with some twenty-five-year-old who was robbing her blind?"

"He's not twenty-five, he's almost thirty. And apparently

Gloria is doing just fine since she bought a condo on Lake Shore and Burton. Two bedrooms, three hundred thousand dollars."

"A hundred and fifty thousand a bedroom?"

"Well, it is an entire floor. And it has more bathrooms than bedrooms."

"How do you know all this?"

"I know her real-estate agent."

"I guess the *Daily Herald* pays better than I thought."

"It doesn't. She acts like she comes from money, but I don't think she does."

"Did they give her a discount for publicity?"

"A steep discount, I imagine."

Another waitress came and asked if we wanted to order lunch. There was wait staff everywhere running around and they didn't seem too concerned with who did what. I ordered the Walnut Room's famous chicken potpie, Sugar ordered a salad, and Brian ordered meatloaf.

When we were alone again, I said, "I'll do a standard background check, but I'd also like to meet France—if you don't think that would be too awkward."

"There's a holiday open house at his studio on Thursday. I've already invited Brian. Come as his guest. Don't mention that I've hired you."

"Of course not. Do you plan to tell him, though? At some point?"

"It depends on what you find."

The conversation drifted to the AIDS test that was supposed to be coming out soon. The test was still being tested, and activists were already raising concerns about confidentiality and whether insurance companies or employers might be able to get hold of your results.

"I was having a conversation with a board member about

creating a testing center where people could be tested for free on a strictly confidential basis," Brian said.

"Does it really matter, though?" I asked. "There's no cure. So what good is knowing?"

"I've heard that before. I think it's better to know. So that people can take precautions."

"People are already taking precautions." Precautions that don't always work, I did not add.

"Darling, it's not just about individuals. The test is also important for research and helping doctors learn how to treat their patients." That was annoyingly true.

Our lunches came. My potpie was mushier than I remembered, but it was warm and tasted like childhood. By dessert the conversation had moved back to Sugar's problems, and I gave her detailed instructions on what departments she should shop in and how long. I planned to give her a head start of about ten minutes, then find her on the first floor in men's cologne, follow her back up to the men's clothing department, and watch her buy a pair of leather gloves and a couple of ties. I wanted to see if anyone was following her. I figured an hour or so would do it.

After Sugar paid for lunch, I checked the old Timex I kept in a pocket of the trench coat Joseph had given me as a joke. It was one forty-five. Brian and I went down to the men's department, while Sugar went down to cosmetics.

"Would it be weird to get my boyfriend school supplies?" I asked. Joseph had signed up for two classes at Loyola. He'd gotten his seminary degree from Niles College, which was affiliated so he'd been able to pick up a couple of classes he thought he'd need if he managed to get accepted into their Social Work program next fall.

"I was kind of particular about my pens and notebooks when I was in school."

"What do you think I should get him, then?"

"Underwear."

"Because no one's particular about underwear?"

"Because you know what kind of underwear he likes, don't you?"

"I know more about what kind of underwear I like to see him in." And they didn't have it at Marshall Field's. I made a mental note that I was going to have to stop by a little boutique called Trunks sometime in the next few days. They had some skimpy briefs in the window, which came in about six colors. Red would look good against his milky—

"What do you think about how Ross is doing?" Brian asked. Ross, who'd once been Brian's boyfriend, was still sleeping in my living room. Well, living in my living room, since he wasn't well enough to go many places.

"I think he's doing remarkably well," I said. "He's eating better and going for walks on his own."

"The other day he said, 'When I get better...'"

"Oh."

That brought me up short. They wouldn't say for sure that everyone who got the AIDS virus would die, but it did seem that was what was happening. And even if everyone didn't die, there wasn't any reason to think that people got better. If anyone was going to make it, they would be the ones who never got too sick. And Ross was already too sick. Finally, I said, "False hope isn't the worst thing in the world, I suppose."

"I guess not. Does Joseph have a bathrobe?"

"Yes."

"What kind?"

"Flannel."

"Good, get him a terry cloth one. They're comfy."

"I don't know. It doesn't feel right."

There were only seven days left before Christmas. I

needed to pick something. Time was running out. Still, I didn't buy a thing.

"You should probably go home," I told Brian.

"What? Why?"

"If Sugar is being followed it will be easier to go unnoticed if it's just me."

"Oh. Okay." He reached over and squeezed my arm. "Um, see you later then."

It felt awkward saying good-bye. If we were girls we could have hugged and kissed each other on the cheek, and we did that at home when I was leaving his apartment or he was leaving mine. But we weren't at home. And we weren't girls. So we made a couple of strange aborted movements toward each other as we said good-bye.

I turned my attention to remembering where I'd told Sugar to be. I went down to the first floor and found men's cologne. Sugar was standing at the counter having a clerk show her everything in the store. She saw me out of the corner of her eye but gave no indication that she knew me. She did stop smelling cologne and had the clerk ring up a pile she had collected. She spent about three hundred and fifty dollars on men's cologne. Nearly as much as I paid in rent. Michael France was going to smell damned good.

I wandered around the department spritzing myself once or twice with testers. There were people everywhere, mostly women. Even though it was crowded, the aisles were filled with gift suggestions: lesser colognes in sets, soap-on-a-rope, comfy corduroy slippers, and travel kits that included clippers and a needle and thread to sew on a button. None of them were things I wanted to give to Joseph.

Most of the first floor was devoted to colognes, perfumes and makeup. For most people these were not necessities, which was why the store made you walk by them. People needed underwear. People needed a new pair of jeans. People needed frying pans. Those things were kept several floors up and deep in the furthest corners. That was the strategy, make you walk by all sorts of things you'd want on your way to things you needed. That pretty much guaranteed you walked out of the store happily carrying more than you'd come for.

Once Sugar was finished checking out, I followed her on the escalator to the second floor men's department. Between us was a dumpy woman from the suburbs carrying three shopping bags. I didn't see anyone suspicious coming down the escalator across from us—well, anyone obviously suspicious.

We reached the second floor. The suburban woman wandered off to shoes, while I followed Sugar around the men's department. The clerk gave me a curious look. I guess people didn't often leave and then come back. I ignored him and kept an eye on Sugar. The men's department was busy, but it was mostly women shopping for Christmas gifts, because what man isn't happy to get two or three new ties each year. What I didn't see was anyone who seemed to be paying attention to Sugar.

I tried not to get closer to Sugar than twenty feet. When she was in casual wear I was in men's suits. When she was in men's underwear I was standing near men's shoes. The suburban woman with the bags had made the clerk bring her a dozen pairs of boy's shoes size 6. She was carefully making a decision.

Sugar had made lots of decisions. By the time she got to the glass case holding leather gloves, she'd bought three Alexander Julian sweaters, two Brooks Brothers shirts, six Izod polo shirts and a comfy looking pair of flannel pajamas. She bought a pair of gloves, as we'd discussed, and then two more pair. Then she went over to the ties and bought a dozen. While the clerk was ringing up her order, Sugar asked to use the phone. After the clerk nodded, she made a call.

She said a few words into the receiver then hung up. Thanking the clerk, she paid for the ties and then, clutching her bags, made her way out of the store.

I held back, scanning the men's department. It didn't seem like anyone was following Sugar. After a few minutes I went downstairs and left the building on the State Street side. Sugar stood at the curb with her bags at her feet and her gloved hands clamping her white fox shut at the neck.

"I didn't see anyone," I said when I got close.

"Darn. And I was hoping to catch them red-handed."

"Who did you call?"

"My driver."

"You have a car phone?"

"Two. One in the front seat and one in the back. You should get one, they're very convenient."

I doubted I had the budget for it. "So, the store just lets people make phone calls like that?"

"Probably not. But when you say, 'I need to call my driver, may I use your phone?' People tend to break rules."

Chapter Two

THE TALK SUGAR and Brian had about testing had unnerved me. Most of the time I was happy—and miserable. I was in love with Joseph, but I knew my love to be selfish. I knew, should have always known, that it was likely I had the virus that caused AIDS, HTLV-III. Meaning I had AIDS. Or would eventually have AIDS. Meaning I could give AIDS. Meaning I had probably given it to him when a thin, seven-inch piece of latex broke nearly two months before.

I took care of a few things at my office and went home to our apartment on Lake Shore Drive. I'd lucked into the cheapest one-bedroom apartment on the lake and now three of us lived there: me, Joseph and Ross. The apartment was probably less than six hundred square feet, had a Pullman kitchen—basically a kitchen in a closet with doors that shut over it—and a killer, fourteen-foot view of Lake Michigan.

When I walked in, Ross was watching *Eyewitness News*. He wore a pair of baby blue pajamas that had probably fit at one point but now made him look like a little boy in his father's clothes. There were lesions on his neck and his lips were always badly chapped, but the freckles across the bridge of his nose and his smile were still the same and managed to lift my spirits.

Linda Yu was explaining that the murder rate for 1984 was one of the highest in years, with gang-related shootings the culprit. Of course, none of the three murders I'd been involved with during the year had anything to do with gangs, but that didn't change the reality of living in Chicago.

"Did you find a present for Joseph?" Ross asked.

"I will."

"You'd better. You only have a week."

The apartment was decorated for Christmas but just barely. I'd had decorations with Daniel, my first lover, but he'd taken the box marked Christmas when he left. I'd bought a few new decorations for the Christmas I'd spent with Bert Harker, but those had gotten lost somewhere along the way. This year, I'd picked some up at Jewel and some at Walgreens, and wondered if maybe I shouldn't show some confidence in the future and buy something fancy at He Who Eats Mud. They had wonderful crystal ornaments in their window, which cost far more than you should ever spend on something you were only going to use for two weeks a year.

Besides, we didn't even have a tree. There wasn't room for one. Instead, we had a bowl of cheap red and green ornaments on the table and a gold and silver garland hung across the window in the living room.

"There's wrapping paper in the closet. You know, for whenever you need it," Ross said, with a smirk on his face. That meant that Joseph had already bought me something and wrapped it.

I gave Ross a good stare and asked, "Am I going to like it?"

"Like what?"

"Whatever you're smirking about."

He shrugged. "I think so."

Keys jangled in the door and Joseph walked in, early. He was working a long-term temp assignment at FirstChicago. They were making this big push to get people to buy IRAs. It was Joseph's job to take a three by five card that someone else had handwritten and type a person's name, address and social security number into a CRT, along with the account number and amount of their deposit. He was very honest about the fact that the hardest thing about the job was staying awake.

"You're early," I said.

"Computers went down." Apparently, they did that a lot. "Nothing to do so they sent me home."

A bit shorter and a few years younger than I am, Joseph's hair was a rusty-brown and, like a lot of people, he'd been growing it out on top. I liked the way it kept falling into his eyes. There was usually a devilish look in those eyes that belied his kind nature. He came over and kissed me. Then he started pushing and pulling me toward the bedroom.

Over his shoulder he said, "Hi Ross! Bye Ross!"

"What are you doing?" I asked as he closed the door behind him.

"What do you think I'm doing?" he asked, undoing the red tie around his neck.

"Kidnapping me?"

"Okay, I'm kidnapping you." He pulled at my gray crew sweater until it popped over my head. Then he kissed me, deeply, making pleasurable little moans as he did. His shirt came off and landed on the floor next to the bed.

We kicked off our shoes and pulled off our pants. I grabbed at his hard dick through his BVDs. Maybe I did want to pick him up a new pack of underwear. Even if it was only tighty-whities. Fresh, crisply white, they looked so good against his skin, so pink and so freckled. He should have a dozen pairs.

He pushed me onto the bed and then climbed on. Framing my face with his hands, he studied me and said, "I love you."

"I love you, too."

I pulled him into a kiss. Then he rolled me on top of him. "I want you to fuck me," he whispered into my ear.

"Not today."

"Nick."

"Don't make it a thing. Let's just have other kinds of fun."

"I'm tired of having other kinds of fun."

Ignoring him, I sat up and yanked his underwear down, enjoying the flop of his dick as I did it. Then I flipped him over, spread his ass cheeks and began to lick his hole.

"You're not helping things," he said, then gasped a couple of times. "That just makes me want—"

They said this might not be safe, but I didn't care. I wasn't the one I was worried about. I couldn't give him anything this way and that was what mattered to me.

When he was good and wet, I slid a finger into him hooking it downward as I did. I moved in and out a few times and then put in another finger. His ass rose up to meet me. I reached beneath him and took hold of his stiff cock.

I knew it wouldn't take long. I'd done it enough times in the last two months to get very, very good at it. Sometimes I did it to him while he lay on his back, and other times, like now, with him on his stomach. It didn't matter. He couldn't get away from me.

He came on the bedspread almost against his will. I scooped up his come and spread it onto my hard prick and jacked off on his creamy white ass.

When I was done he rolled over and said, "You're a terrible man, Nick Nowak."

"I am. I am a terrible man."

But not because I wouldn't fuck him. I was a terrible man because I'd taken his love, taken the happiness he had to give, and in return I had possibly, probably, given him an early death. I couldn't know, of course. Couldn't be sure. Not until they started giving people the test—and God knows when that would happen. They said spring. But it could be summer. Or fall. Or not at all.

Of course, I might not have given him the virus. Or I might have. Happiness and misery had become bound together.

"Don't think about it," Joseph said.

"How do you know what I'm thinking about?"

"How could I not know? You're thinking about it all the time." Then he said what he'd said before. "Nick, a condom broke. It happens."

"You want me to pretend it never happened?"

"A little bit of denial isn't a bad think, Nick."

I'd said pretty much the same thing to Brian about Ross just a few hours before. While I should probably have been agreeing with him, I didn't want to. I wanted to be contrary, so I said, "Is that what your therapist says?"

"Yes, as a matter of fact it is what my therapist says."

Joseph had started therapy about six weeks before. I wasn't crazy about it. I knew it was part of his becoming a therapist someday. It was just a part I wished he could skip.

"So you told him about the condom breaking?" I asked.

"Yes."

"And you tell him what you're up to on cheat day?"

"Yes, I tell him what I do on Fridays."

We were quiet for a bit. I hated the idea that there was this person, this Donald Herrington, who sat in an office down in Lincoln Park and listened to my lover tell him things that I didn't know. Eventually, Joseph asked, "Do you want to know what I do on Fridays?"

"Do you want to know what I do on Fridays?" I asked, reflexively.

"Not really. I don't see the point. But…if you want to know what I do I'll tell you. And you don't have to tell me."

"That doesn't seem fair."

"It doesn't have to be fair. It has to be the way we want it to be. And, I don't really want to know what you're up to. What do you want?"

"I don't know. I don't know what I want."

"If you want to know I'll tell you everything. But you have to be sure. I can't un-tell you."

We'd had this conversation before in various forms. I didn't care for it and I wanted to stop having it. I hated talking about things I wasn't sure of. And I really didn't know if I wanted to know what Joseph was doing. Well, maybe that's not right. I wanted to know. But I wanted to know that he wasn't having all that much fun, that there wasn't that much there for him to learn, that he was learning that it was all a big mistake.

Those were stupid things to want, though, because I knew that sometimes catting around was really fun, knew that there was always something to learn, and seriously doubted he was making a mistake.

It was my job to know things, though. To help people know things. And, in the end, that is what always stopped me from asking him to tell me. I knew from experience that knowing the truth could be a dangerous thing. And, very often, when you finally learned what the truth really was, you didn't want to know it.

Chapter Three

IN OCTOBER, Vincent Renaldi began calling me. I'd met him years ago working on a failed political campaign, and that had led to Peterson-Palmer being a client for roughly three years. Things went sideways in late 1982 and I lost the gig. Now, two years later, he was calling me. I had a little trouble returning the call. When I finally got back to him in mid-November he was at the end of his rope.

"Nick, you have to meet me."

"About?"

"Things with your replacement aren't working out."

"So, fire him and hire me back," I said, a little boldly. I'd recently ended my association with Jimmy English; Owen Lovejoy, Esquire; and the firm of Cooke, Babcock and Lackerby; which left me needing a bit of steady work.

"It's a her and we need talk."

"Do you want me to come to your office?"

"I don't know if that's a good idea."

This was getting weirder by the second.

"Do you want to come to my office?"

"You're in New Town, right? I can't be gone that long."

"Why don't you meet me for lunch at the French Bakery? It's near FirstChicago."

He agreed, so we met there the next day. The French Bakery was where Brian worked and where Ross had also worked for a short while. I used to spend a fair amount of time there when my office was on LaSalle. It's a cute little place with take-out downstairs, real French bakers making the croissants, a busy happy hour, and a very reasonable lunch menu.

I forget what day of the week it was that Vincent and I finally met, but it was busy. Even though I tried to sit in Brian's section, the only place they could seat us was in the overflow dining room in the very back. Our waitress was a nervous little blond girl who was swimming in her black slacks, white shirt and butcher's apron.

"Can I, uh, get you something from the bar?" My bet was she hoped we wouldn't want anything since the bar was at the complete other end of the restaurant.

"I'll have a Beefeater Martini with a twist. Straight up," Vincent said.

To be sociable, I ordered a Johnnie Walker Red on the rocks. She walked away and I stared at Vincent, waiting for him to say something. I hadn't seen him in years, but he hadn't changed all that much. He was a small, wiry man with a heavy beard, dark hair that would soon be salt and pepper, and coal black eyes. He still wore a thick mustache and, I suspected, was still fond of black leather in his off hours.

"I'm sorry I had to let you go two years ago," he finally said.

"It was a bad time for me. So I'll forgive you."

"Oh, no, I didn't mean that kind of sorry. I meant, I'm sorry for *me*. Letting you go hasn't worked out well."

He seemed in a bad place so I cut him some slack. "I wouldn't have been able to keep working for you anyway.

You didn't have a lot of choices. Now, tell me about this woman who's working for you."

"Lindquist Investigations. Have you heard of them?"

"No." I didn't happen to know *any* other private investigators, for that matter. It wasn't like there was a special bar where we went to hang out, sip beer, and exchange trade secrets—or, if there was, I didn't know about it. I'd gotten my license based on my years with the CPD, so I hadn't even had to do an apprenticeship with another investigator.

"A woman named Rita Lindquist owns it. It used to be her father's, but he got lung cancer."

"So what's the problem?"

"I don't think she's doing a very good job."

"Why do you think that?"

"Right after she started we hired a man named Bill Appleton and, well, let's just say he's not working out. I'd like you to do your regular check on him and we'll compare it to what Lindquist did. That way we'll get some idea what she's up to."

"If you don't trust her, you should just fire her."

He hedged. "I feel like I need actual proof."

Our drinks arrived and he took a long swallow of his. I sipped mine. We told the waitress we'd order in a bit.

"So, tell me everything you know about this Lindquist woman."

"She's bold, brash, the things she wears aren't appro—"

"Why did you hire her?"

"I didn't have much choice."

"She went over your head?"

"Yeah, that's what happened. Exactly."

Something about the way he said that made me feel like I'd guessed wrong. I knew better than that, too. I knew I should just get him talking and keep my big mouth shut.

I took another stab at it, "Tell me more."

"Well, you know the job. You don't need to come into the office at all, really. I messenger you the information and you get to work. But Rita, she's always coincidentally in the neighborhood. Or she's made friends with one of the secretaries and they're going to lunch. Or she was bored and wanted to get out of her office. That's why I didn't want to meet at the office. She always seems to be there."

"Where's her office?"

"By the river. That new building." The river was a good fifteen, sixteen blocks away from Peterson-Palmer. She wouldn't often be in the neighborhood.

"So she's friendly with other people in the office?"

"Yes. A lot of them."

"Married or single?"

"Single. Well, not exactly single. I think she's involved with Bill Appleton."

"Why do you think that?"

The waitress came back and asked again if we were ready to order. She hadn't given us much time but we were polite enough to order anyway. Vincent chose a roast beef sandwich au jus on French bread and I picked the quiche of the day. Spinach and mushroom. They say real men don't eat quiche, but since most of the world doesn't consider me a real man I say fuck it. I eat quiche.

After the girl walked away, I repeated my question, "Why do you think Rita's involved with this Appleton guy?"

"She's in his office a lot. They go to lunch."

"We're at lunch, we're not having an affair."

"I don't know that they go to a restaurant, though."

"So Appleton's not working out. Inept or criminal?"

"I'm not sure. That's one of the things we have to find out."

And that was all the business we did. After that, we gossiped about a politician we both knew and talked about the general state of the world, which we agreed was not good. They'd put a baboon heart into a baby and wondered why that didn't work out; John Lennon was still releasing records, even though he'd been dead four years; and McDonald's has sold 50 billion hamburgers. Obviously the end of the world was near.

I spent the next week putting together my background check on William B. Appleton. He was thirty-six years old (when I checked the information he'd provided that proved to be correct). According to his resume, he wasn't originally from the area. The Loop, and Peterson-Palmer in particular, was populated by graduates of Wheaton, Northwestern, Loyola, University of Chicago and the occasional over-achiever from ISU down in Normal. Appleton listed the Anderson School of Business at UCLA. That alone made him unusual.

I called 213-555-1212 and got the general number for UCLA. After being bounced around a few times I finally got to the registrar, but it turned out to be worth my time and the cost of the long distance call. Appleton had not gone the Anderson School at all. He had attended UCLA as a freshman and sophomore, but that was it. That was the extent of his education at UCLA. He was a dropout. I did have to admit that it wasn't a bad idea to say you graduated from a school you'd actually attended. If push came to shove and you ran into a fellow alumni, you could at least reminisce about how bad the cafeteria food was.

After that, I looked closely at his work experience. He claimed to have been a financial planner at a Lincoln Savings and Loan in North Long Beach, California, right after he didn't graduate from business school. Another call to directory assistance confirmed my suspicion that there was no such office. There were similar problems with his next two supposed jobs. To make himself look good, he stayed at each phony job for a little over two years. Each title was a tiny bit better and there were no crazy jumps in status or mysterious gaps.

If I were doing a regular check, I'd have stopped there and called Renaldi. A phony degree and a couple of fake jobs was enough to get a person bounced from a firm like Peterson-Palmer. Before working at Peterson-Palmer, Appleton had worked at another financial company in the Loop: Becker, Fleet and O'Day. I could have called there to check him out, but I wanted to be careful word that I was looking into him did not get back to him. You never know who's friends with whom.

Something was bothering me, though. It had only taken me a few minutes to figure out that this guy was wrong for Peterson-Palmer, so why had Rita Lindquist given him a pass? Had she simply not done anything on his file? Or was something else going on? And, if she was having a relationship with Appleton, had it begun before he started at Peterson-Palmer? Or after?

I spent a morning down at the county clerk's office doing a record search. I discovered that Appleton married Doreen Siemanski in a religious ceremony presided over by a minister named Jeremiah Robinson on June 14, 1978. That didn't exactly jibe with his resume, which didn't have Appleton residing in Cook County until 1980 when he took the job at Becker, Fleet and O'Day.

I also learned that Bill and Doreen owned a condominium on Cornelia, a block from the Drive. The address was the same as on Bill's resume, which probably made it the most honest thing he put down. They'd lived there since 1979. Also, before he'd supposedly moved to Chicago.

Having done about as much as I could with public records, I took a 146 express bus from downtown up to Belmont and then hung out for a few more stops until we got to Cornelia. Something told me I'd learn a lot from Mrs. Appleton. I just had to be sure she didn't tip off her husband.

The building was the second one in on the south side of the street. It was probably twenty stories tall, with balconies on each end and windows that popped out at an angle to improve homeowners' view of the lake. Pacing in front, I tried to think of a way to get information from Mrs. Appleton without tipping my hand.

The thing that was tricky was that I didn't know her attitude toward her husband. Did she hate him? Did she still love him? Was she resigned and ambivalent? I wished I could simply choose what her attitude was toward her husband. It would make things much easier. Then I realized I might be able to do exactly that if I just fudged a little on the legalities.

I entered the lobby of the building and brazenly walked by the doorman. You usually could if you acted like you lived there. I knew that Doreen lived in 12F, so I went straight to the elevator and pressed 12. The doors were closing and I was on my way before the doorman thought twice about me.

When I reached the twelfth floor I easily found apartment F. Beyond the door someone had a TV on, so I knew that Mrs. Appleton was home. I took my gloves off and shoved them into my trench coat pockets. Then I opened the coat so I wouldn't sweat to death. I slumped my shoulders, hung my head and knocked.

A moment later, a pretty young woman in a pink leotard and black tights opened the door. On the TV behind her Jane Fonda was doing aerobics. She looked me up and down and said, "You'd better not be trying to sell me something 'cause we don't let people do that here."

"I'm, uh." I should have made up a name before I knocked. "I'm Rita Lindquist's fiancé."

Her face got hard. "Are you?"

"Are you Doreen? I wanted, um, I was hoping we could talk. No one else knows what I've been going through."

I looked down and squeezed the bridge of my nose with two fingers as though I were struggling not to cry. I pulled myself together and looked at her.

"You poor thing," she said. "You'd better come in."

She stepped back, opening the door wider. I walked into the apartment.

"Can I get you something to drink? I have eggnog, believe it or not. Don't have any; it'll make you sick as a dog. I'm saving it for my husband."

"I'll just have a glass of water if it's no trouble."

She gave me a compassionate look and went into the kitchen. The exercise video continued to play. On the console television there were a half dozen photographs next to a Betamax. Five of them were of Doreen following various athletic pursuits: hiking, climbing, swimming and long distance running. The last photo was a fairly traditional wedding photo of Doreen and an attractive, brown-haired guy in his mid-twenties. They looked happy.

When she came back with the glass of water, I asked, "Is this your husband?"

"Of course it is. I don't wear a white dress for just any guy. I'd throw the picture away but I look really good in it." She was right. She did look good in the photo.

"How long have you known?" she asked.

"Almost a month," I said. It was a guess. I had no idea how long the affair had been going on. Or how long she'd known.

"A month? But he moved in with Rita almost a year ago."

"I've been away."

"Prison?" she guessed.

"Pipeline. Alaska." I knew there was a pipeline up that way, Of course, it might have gotten finished years ago.

"Oh, I see. Well, this is quite a mess to come back to."

"You said you're saving the eggnog for your husband?"

"He comes around every so often and tries to get me to move out of the condo. My lawyer has given me strict instructions not to budge. After awhile he gives up and tries to have sex with me."

"You don't have sex with him, do you?"

"No. I'm tempted. You know, do to Rita what she did to me. But I can't go through with it now that I know what a lowlife he is."

"He's a lowlife?"

"Oh yeah, my lawyer found all sorts of things on him. Do you have a lawyer yet?"

"No. We're not married. We were supposed to get married in two months."

"Oh, that's right. Fiancé, you said?"

"Yes, that's what I said."

"Bill never mentioned you."

"I'm not surprised. What kinds of things did your lawyer find out?"

"You don't need to know."

"But I'm sure if Rita knew she'd—"

"She'd come back to you? Sorry to be the one to tell you, but Rita knows." Then she looked at me funny. "She's a private investigator, she knows everything."

"Well, yeah, I know what she does for a living but, I mean, she says it's boring, that she's always looking things up at the country clerk and looking through old newspapers."

"Uh-huh," Doreen said. I didn't think she was buying it, though the job was usually kind of boring. "That's how they fell in love. She was investigating him."

"Isn't that against the rules. Can't she get disbarred or something like that?"

"Yeah, I don't think it's the most ethical profession." I

decided not to take offense to that. "What did you say your name was?"

"Harold," I said, the first name that popped into my mind. "Wa—Warren." I'd almost said Washington. Harold Washington. That would have made a real mess of things.

"Well, Harold," she said. "Do you feel better?"

"Excuse me?"

"You said you wanted to talk to someone who knows what you're going through."

"Yes, thank you for that." I offered her the empty glass. "I really should be going."

"Yeah, I gotta get back to my workout. Are you exercising? It helps you know."

"Does it?"

"You won't believe it."

I walked toward the door. She came with me. Once I was safely in the hallway she said, "Um, I don't know who you really are or what you're up to, but I hope you nail the bitch."

Chapter Four

AFTER MY MEETING with Doreen Appleton nee Sieman-ski, I called Vincent. He wasn't in so I left a message with his secretary that he should call. He didn't. For the first few days, I thought fair is fair. I took forever to answer his calls, so I chalked it up to karma. He did keep sending me work, four or five candidates a week for me to check out. I imagine he was paying Rita to do to the same work, but that was his problem.

Something was off about the whole thing. If Doreen was right, Rita had been doing a background check on Bill Appleton and when he failed, instead of turning him in she fell for him. Which said a whole lot about what kind of a person Rita Lindquist was. None of it very nice.

A lot of Vincent's behavior was unusual to say the least. Why had he hired her? Why didn't he fire her? And why wasn't he calling me back? Finally, I wrote up my report and sent it to him with an up-to-date invoice.

The morning after my shopping trip at Field's, he finally called me. "I'm sorry, believe it or not, this is our busy season. People leave their yearly planning until the end of the year when they can't do much about it."

That was probably true, but I didn't know what it would have to do with Human Resources. I doubt they expected him to hire and fire people faster due to the busy season.

"So, do you want me to come down?"

"No. Can you meet me for a drink at The Loading Zone?"

I rolled my eyes but said, "What time?"

"Five thirty?

"Sure, why not?"

I hung up and turned my attention to Michael France. The first thing I wanted to do was a bit on the tedious side. I stacked up every single *Daily Herald* I had, which was about three months worth, and then I read "The Silver Spoon" column and put aside each and every mention of Michael France.

In three months, Gloria Silver had mentioned Michael France eighteen times. Ten times she mentioned that he'd chaperoned her to this place or that, but those mentions were in the older editions. There was one picture of them together at a formal benefit for My Old Friend, a charity that provided services for the elderly. Gloria looked thin and elegant, as though she was most comfortable in a strapless gown. She was dyeing her hair blonder than when I last saw her. Or, perhaps she'd let it go silver to match the column and her name. I couldn't tell since the photos were black-and-white newsprint.

The more recent mentions of France were that he'd sold a painting to a socialite in Lake Forest; that he was opening a show in Cincinnati next spring; and that the most decadent thing he'd ever bought for himself was a thousand-dollar bottle of wine, which he claimed was worth every penny.

Just to be thorough, I went through the papers again and

this time looked for mentions of Sugar in the columns. Sugar had fewer mentions in the last three months, only twelve. Most of them were recent. A number of the mentions were just additions to lists of people who'd attended parties. One called her an outright drunk, which was shocking since Gloria typically saved those accusations for her blind items. Two mentioned Sugar having secret rendezvous with more than one man.

There was one mention of both Sugar and France, which reported that she'd bought one of France's paintings and even said—almost out of character for Gloria—that with Sugar's seal of approval he was bound to sell paintings to everyone who was anyone in Chicago.

When all was said and done, Gloria's coverage of Sugar was a little all over the map. On Tuesday she hated her and by Thursday she seemed to have forgiven her. It was definitely schizophrenic.

I knew I had to go downtown to do the basics on France: marriage records, property records, etc. One of Gloria's articles made reference to his attending art school in London and having been a fixture on the New York art scene. So, he probably wasn't a Chicagoan, which meant there would be fewer records on him, if any. I wanted to put it off but knew I shouldn't.

I decided to wait until the afternoon, since I could swing back to The Loading Zone when I was done. In this weather, the last thing I wanted to do was go to the Loop, come back to Boystown, and then go back down to Oak Street. I'd spend half my day traveling through slush.

There wasn't a whole lot to do, so I just sat at my desk and pondered—well, I lit a cigarette and pondered. What kind of a man goes from Gloria Silver to Sugar Pilson? The two women had more in common than not. Both were attractive, powerful, well-known, well-connected women.

Sugar was roughly in her mid-to-late thirties, while Gloria was a decade older. Gloria was a terrible person, while Sugar was decent, kind and generous—but also someone I wouldn't want to cross.

That made Michael France a man who liked powerful women, women who could advance his career. Assuming Sugar wasn't simply a step up, what could she do that Gloria couldn't? In order to sell five-thousand-dollar paintings, France needed access to rich people. Both Gloria and Sugar provided that in roughly the same measure. In fact, taking a strictly mercenary view, Gloria was the better choice—

My phone rang.

"Hi," Joseph said, when I picked up.

"Hi." We tried to call each other every day.

"How's your day going?"

"I have a meeting at five-thirty, so I don't think I'll be home until around seven, seven-thirty."

"Okay, I'll feed Ross and wait for you." Ross needed to eat at specific times so he could take his meds with food.

"No, you go ahead and eat. I'll have leftovers."

Ignoring me, he said, "So, I was thinking about Christmas."

"What about it?"

"I want to have it together."

"Oh."

That was a surprise. Joseph hadn't told his family he was no longer a priest and I hadn't told Mrs. Harker, my sort of semi-mother-in-law, that I was living with someone who had given her communion on more than one occasion. At Thanksgiving we'd dealt with these problems by going our separate ways: I'd gone to Mrs. Harker's and Joseph had spent the day with his family.

"I think I can fit a twelve-pound bird in the oven, or

maybe we should do ham? What did you have when you were a kid?"

On Christmas Eve we had a Polish dinner of borscht, pierogies and herring. On Christmas Day we had an American Christmas of turkey with the usual trimmings.

"We had turkey," I told him, deliberately leaving out Christmas Eve dinner for fear he'd try to replicate it. I liked my heritage, but that didn't mean I could stomach it.

Of course, Joseph's family was Polish, too. Just not *as* Polish. Poles came to Chicago starting in the middle of the eighteen hundreds and continued to come in droves until the Depression. Joseph's family arrived right after the Civil War, while mine showed up in Chicago right before World War I. His family had an extra fifty years to forget the old country. Not to mention his mother was Irish.

"So does this mean you're telling your parents you're not a priest anymore and that you've moved in with me and that you're—"

"Gay. Yes."

"Isn't that a lot to spring on them at one time?" I asked.

"I need to start having an honest relationship with them." That sounded like his therapist talking.

"I don't think people have honest relationships with their parents."

"Nick."

"All right. It's up to you," I said, even though it put me in a spot with Mrs. Harker.

"Thanks."

"When are you telling them?"

"You have a thing tomorrow night, don't you?"

"I do."

"I'll do it then." We were quiet a moment, then he added, "This isn't going to be as bad as we think."

No, I thought, *it's going to be worse.*

MY INCLINATION WAS to wait and call Mrs. Harker on Christmas morning and tell her I was puking my guts out. But the idea that she might be alone with a ridiculous amount of food on Christmas Day seemed wrong. I put it off for ten minutes before I bit the bullet and called her.

Terry answered the phone.

"What are you doing home?" I asked. It was a school day.

"Mrs. Harker has a stomach thing."

I didn't exactly trust that since he'd lied to me about it before. I asked, "Can she come to the phone?"

Like the sullen teenager he was, Terry simply dropped the phone on the counter and started yelling, "Mrs. Harker! Phone!"

After a long wait, I heard, "Hello? Who is calling please?"

"It's Nick. How do you feel, Mrs. Harker?"

"I need to go to doctor."

"Okay. When?"

"Now. You come."

And then she hung up.

I grabbed my trench coat, scarf and gloves. I was not excited about driving to Edison Park. It was hovering around thirty degrees and had been raining a bit, so driving was going to be slow and tedious.

And it was.

It took nearly an hour and fifteen minutes to get to Mrs. Harker's condo. I hoped this wasn't a big deal. That she hadn't actually needed an ambulance. Or if she had that she'd also had enough sense to call one and not wait for me. I'd spent roughly seventeen months with Bert Harker, but the relationship cast a long shadow and his mother was part of that shadow. At first she hated me, then loathed me, then needed me, until finally we'd established a prickly sort of friendship. I wasn't ready to lose it.

She must have been waiting in the lobby outside her apartment, because as soon as I pulled up in the Versailles—it was kind of a spoiled-peach color and hard to miss—she came out of the building. She didn't look too bad, a little older than she had a week ago, but that happened sometimes. The elderly had aging spurts, just like teenagers had growing spurts.

I leaned over the passenger seat and pushed the door open for her. She climbed in. We didn't say hello, we just sat for a minute. Finally, I asked, "Where is your doctor?"

"I don't have doctor. I go to Swedish lady in Andersville."

"Andersonville," I corrected her.

"Yes. Is what I say."

I struggled to decode what she was saying. It sounded like being Swedish automatically made you an M.D. Still, I asked, "Is that where you want to go? To the Swedish lady?"

"No, I want doctor."

"Do you want to go to the emergency room?"

"Hospital? No, no, I don't want to go to hospital. Doctor is fine."

"What doctor?"

"Your doctor."

"Oh."

This was kind of crazy. Didn't she know that you had to make an appointment to see a doctor?

"When was the last time you went to the doctor?" I asked.

"I don't remember. I don't like doctor."

"Okay. You saw a doctor when you had Bert, didn't you?"

"No. I have midwife." That sounded primitive.

"What do you do when you have a bad cold or an infection?"

"I go to Swedish lady. She give drops." I think that meant the Swedish lady was a homeopath.

I pulled away from the curb. I doubted I'd be able to get her in to see Dr. Macht, but once there I might be able to persuade her to make an appointment. And then we could do all of this again in a week or two.

Dr. Macht's office, which he shared with his lover, was all the way back in Boystown on Halsted. An hour later, we parked in front of a three-story, white building taking up half a block. Drs. Macht and Locklear had offices on the second floor. I helped Mrs. Harker up the two flights of stairs and walked into the reception area. Decorated in pastel blue and mauve, the waiting room had uncomfortable chairs and a comfortable-looking couch, which was already filled with waiting patients. The patients were mainly gay men and there was a table boasting brochures about syphilis, gonorrhea and hepatitis. I hoped Mrs. Harker didn't pay much attention to it.

I went up to the receptionists' window and smiled. "We don't have an appointment, but I'm wondering if you could squeeze us in to see Dr. Macht?"

The woman who was a bit younger than I was and very serious said, "Oh dear. Are you a patient of Dr. Macht?"

"I am, but it's actually my friend who needs to see him. And she hasn't been before."

She lifted herself off her chair a little so she could get a look at Mrs. Harker, who'd taken a seat behind me. "What seems to be the trouble?"

"Oh. I think she's having stomach issues." I'd ridden with her all the way in on the Kennedy and hadn't been able to pry out any more information about what was wrong with her.

"I could get you in Wednesday, the day after Christmas."

"If that's all you can do, we'll take it but..." I leaned in.

"She hasn't been to a doctor in decades. If she feels better by then, she won't come back."

She looked at me for a moment. "Really? Decades?"

"Decades."

"Okay. Let's do both. I'll put you down for next Wednesday at two o'clock. And I'll go see if we can get you in today for at least a few minutes. What's the name?"

"Eva Harker."

She looked at me again. This time she recognized me. "Oh, you're Bert Harker's friend. He was such a nice man."

"Yes. This is his mother."

"Well, yes, of course we want to take care of her." She handed me a clipboard with some xeroxed forms. "Why don't you fill these out and I'll go push some people around."

She slid the glass window shut. I walked over to Mrs. Harker, handed her the clipboard, and said, "You need to fill this out."

"What for is this?"

"They need information about you."

"They not talk to me?"

"They want to do both. They get more information this way."

She pursed her lips and reluctantly began to work on the form. After a minute or two, she stopped and then pointed at a list of ailments.

"How I know?" she asked.

I looked at the list. Of course she didn't know if she had heart disease or diabetes or thyroid problems, since she hadn't been to a doctor in forever.

"You don't know. That's your answer."

She kept at it. Before she finished a stocky, short-haired girl in scrubs opened the door and said, "Eva Harker?"

Mrs. Harker got up and began to walk toward the nurse. Part way there she stopped, turned around and looked at me.

"You come."

"That's okay. I'll wait here."

"You don't leave me alone with strange man."

"If you're uncomfortable you can ask that the nurse be there.

"Ha! Nurse is maybe duke."

Duke? What was—oh shit, she meant dyke. And she said it right in front of the girl, too.

I stood up to follow. Mrs. Harker turned around and continued into the exam area. I looked at the nurse and rolled my eyes. She smiled at me. She probably saw worse than Mrs. Harker every day. Well, maybe just once a week.

"You're in exam room D."

"D? Where is D?" Mrs. Harker asked.

"Next door on your right."

A moment later, the three of us were in a small exam room with a tiny sink, a bulky exam table and a couple of cabinets. The nurse had a file with her. She opened it up on the counter and made a few notes. Then she took Mrs. Harker's blood pressure, temperature, pulse, and asked her to stand on a scale. She wrote down the results.

Then, she handed Mrs. Harker a gown and said, "Can you put this on, Eva." It was definitely not a question.

Mrs. Harker looked at it and said, "Is too small."

The nurse looked nonplussed. To the uninitiated Mrs. Harker looked like a sweet old lady.

"I'll deal with this," I told the nurse.

"Thank you." She walked out of the room.

"Look, the doctor is going to need to… uh, feel around. That's why they want—"

"No. That why you here. You make him stop."

"Okay, you're wearing a girdle, right?"

"We don't talk about such things."

"If there's something wrong with you he can't feel it

through a girdle. I'm going to step into the hallway. Take your undergarments off and if you won't wear the gown put your dress back on."

She gave me a filthy look as I stepped into the hallway. I really wanted to step outside and have a cigarette, but I didn't think slipping out of a girdle would take long enough. I leaned against the wall with my arms crossed.

Dr. Macht walked up, a folder open in his hand. He was reading, so he didn't see me at first. He was a few years younger than me, had a big beard and a head of shaggy hair that needed to be trimmed.

"Oh, hello," he said, when he finally looked up.

"Hello, Dr. Macht."

"It's Nick, isn't it? What are you doing here? You're not on my schedule."

"I've brought in Bert's mother."

"What's going on?"

"She's having some stomach problems. And she hasn't been to a doctor in a very long time. She's been seeing a Swedish woman in Andersonville."

"Oh yes, I've heard about the Swedish woman. She's a homeopath."

"Does that work?"

"It's hard to tell. Some of my patients feel it works for them and maybe it does. And if it doesn't work, well, it's harmless. Of course, I wouldn't go to the Swedish woman with a broken bone."

A terrible feeling sloshed around in my stomach. The fact that we weren't seeing the Swedish woman meant something. It meant Mrs. Harker had something bad and she knew it.

He knocked on the door and Mrs. Harker said we could enter. She stood in the center of the room with her dress hanging around her. Her belt and a stack of dingy undergarments sat on a chair. Without her undergarments she looked more like a woman and less like a tank.

"Hello, Mrs. Harker, I'm Dr. Macht. I treated your son Bert."

"Yes," she said, scowling.

"I liked him very much."

She didn't say anything. Just more scowling.

"All right, why don't you hop up on the table and we can get started."

I helped her onto the table. Dr. Macht listened to her heart through the thin dress. Then he asked her to lie down.

"I understand you're having some stomach pain? Can you show me where?"

She moved her hand around her lower abdomen. Dr. Macht gently explored that area. "Are you experiencing any nausea or vomiting?"

"No."

"Does this hurt?"

She grunted but said, "No."

"Are you having any pain in your back?"

"I work hard. Clean floors myself."

"I'm sure you do. So you're having pain in your back, but you think it comes from cleaning?"

"Yes."

"Can you open your dress? I should examine your breasts."

"No. You not do."

Dr. Macht looked at me. I shrugged.

"I could have the nurse come in and do it for me, if you like."

"I do not like, no."

"We're going to have to examine your breasts at some point. We can skip it for today, but it needs to happen."

"We skip."

Then, he felt around her neck and jaw, under her arms and finally tried to give a bit more attention to her pelvic area. He explored a little too long and she said, "Enough."

"You've brought Nick with you, is it all right if I talk to him about your case?"

She shrugged like it was an insignificant question.

"Okay, we're going to take care of a few things and while we're gone you can put your things back on.

Dr. Macht and I left the exam room. He led me to a busy nurses' area. He waved at the nurse Mrs. Harker had called a duke and leaned close to her giving her some instructions. Then, he stepped back over to me.

"She's quite a character."

"She is."

"I did feel some kind of growth on or near her left ovary. It could be benign. I may have felt some swelling in her lymph nodes although that's harder to pick up in a physical exam. I'm getting you set up with X-rays—lungs, pelvis, colon—a CAT scan with contrast of the pelvic area, and a mammogram. How much pain do you think she's in?"

"Well, we're here so I'd say a lot."

"Yes, she seemed to be in pain while I was examining her. I'm going to prescribe some Darvon. She should at least take them at night so that she sleeps well. I'm also going to give you half a dozen Valium. You keep those. Try to get her to take one before you go in for the mammogram. She'll be more…receptive."

"Can we give her one now?" I joked.

He smiled and said, "There's a Walgreens across the street if you want to fill these while I talk to her."

"Thanks."

I left the building and walked across the street. My head was a little foggy. This all sounded serious, which complicated my life quite a bit. The reason I'd called Mrs. Harker in the first place had been to cancel Christmas dinner. But I couldn't do that now. I couldn't let her spend the day alone. I didn't want to disappoint Joseph, either. But she was sick and I couldn't—

I handed the prescriptions over to the pharmacist. They'd take a few minutes, so I went and looked at magazines. Brazenly, I picked up *Playgirl*. The Australian actor Mel Gibson was on the cover but fully clothed inside—such a waste. There were a couple of other so-called celebrity nudes: the guy who'd done *Flash Gordon* and a soap opera actor looking for more exposure. The centerfold was an uninspiring French guy. There were articles, too, but I didn't have the patience to even read the titles.

I was going to have to go to Mrs. Harker's for Christmas dinner, I decided. But then I thought about all the work she'd have to do and I didn't want her cooking that much. Not if she was in pain. So, then I decided she'd have to come have Christmas dinner with us. That was a terrible idea. She didn't know about Joseph and she'd probably hate him, and then me, and it just sounded awful. All my options were awful. I just had to decide which awful thing I was going to do for the holiday. The pharmacist called out "Harker" and I went and paid for the prescriptions.

Walking back into Dr. Macht's office, I found Mrs. Harker in the waiting room. In her hand was the information for tests she needed. I took the sheets and glanced at them. X-rays were on Friday. The CAT scan Christmas Eve and the mammogram on the 26th. Dr. Macht had been kind enough to set them up in order of difficulty.

As we left, Mrs. Harker seemed particularly prickly. And I certainly couldn't begrudge her that; she'd just received some very difficult news. I didn't feel like I had much choice but to say, "You should come to my place for Christmas dinner."

"No. You and boy you come. I cook."

"I don't want you going to all that trouble."

"Is not trouble. Is dinner."

"No, I want you to come to my place. You can make one dish."

She didn't look happy about it, but she went quiet. As we got on the Kennedy again, she asked, "What is be-nine?"

"It means harmless."

"Oh. I see." Her mood lifted immediately, as though the doctor hadn't used words like might and could and possibly, words I'm sure he used and she did not hear.

Chapter Five

I DROPPED MRS. HARKER OFF, turned around and drove back to Boystown. It was getting late, so I parked near my apartment and caught the 146 Express bus without going inside. There was no way in hell I was driving my car down to Oak Street. Even though the bus was going against rush hour traffic, I arrived about ten minutes late.

The Loading Zone was in the basement of a building that also housed an expensive leather goods shop and a trendy hair stylist. I hadn't been in years. I used to go all the time when my office was in the Loop. When I walked down the stairs, sinking below the sidewalk, I found that the bar was just as packed and just as smoky as ever. The jukebox was playing "Do They Know It's Christmas," which was every-where just then. The record was meant to benefit starving people in Africa, which may have escaped the guys in bar singing along.

I lit a cigarette and looked around for Vincent. He was a small, wiry man with a heavy beard, dark hair and coal black eyes. He usually wore a thick mustache and, in his off hours, had an affection for black leather. It took about five minutes, but I finally spotted him wedged between the cigarette machine and a gangly blond. He still had the mustache, and had let his hair grow out so that it was long in the back, long on top and tightly cropped on the sides. His hair was curly like mine was when it grew out. I could have gotten a cut like his, but it reminded me too much of a poodle.

He saw me, said something to the blond, and came over.

"Thank you for coming," he said.

"Let me get a drink," I said. "Do you need one?"

"Stoli and tonic," he said.

I tried to move toward the bar but got jostled a couple of times. I turned to Vincent and told him, "Find some place out of the way."

I got the drinks while he claimed a spot in the corner. When I got to him, he practically snatched his drink out of my hand.

"You haven't been completely honest with me, have you, Vincent?"

"Why would you say something like that?"

"You have every reason in the world to fire Rita Lindquist and you haven't done it yet."

"She's a woman, so it's a little more delicate."

"It's only more delicate if you want to fire her for being a woman. You can fire her for doing bad work and you have a lot of back up on that score."

"I wouldn't say a lot."

"I would say letting one bad apple into your financial bushel is enough."

He finished his drink. I'd barely taken two sips of mine. I didn't offer to go get him another. Instead, I just kept staring at him. Finally, I said, "Tell me again about how Rita got the job. Who was it that made you hire her?"

"I wasn't completely honest about that. Nobody made me hire her."

"So, why did you?"

"I didn't have a choice."

"Yeah, I remember you saying that. Why didn't you have a choice?"

"You know, she just showed up one day. I hadn't even started looking to replace you and there she was. She said she wanted the job and to show how much she'd already done her first background check. On me."

I had a bad feeling about where this might be going. "What did she find?"

"About two and a half years ago, I got picked up for having sex in Lincoln Park."

There were lots of places in Lincoln Park to have sex, if you didn't mind grass stains. I have to admit I've found sex in the park a couple of times myself.

"That's a misdemeanor," I said. And, no, I hadn't found that out the hard way.

Misdemeanors didn't always show up on background checks, and even when they did employers didn't often care. If he had a misdemeanor for exposure he could always say he was drunk and peeing on a wall—the details of an arrest were seldom included so you could talk your way out of it.

I hadn't quite finished thinking all of that when he said, "No. It's worse than that. The guy I was having sex with turned out to be sixteen."

"You didn't ask how old he was?"

"Really, Nick? It was two in the morning. What was a sixteen-year-old kid doing cruising the park? Where were his parents?"

He was right. People should keep their sixteen-year-olds where they could see them. Brian and I had had our hands full with Terry. He'd made the occasional attempt at seducing older men, so it didn't surprise me that kids would do whatever they can get away with.

At the same time, I understood enough about the law to know that the responsibility was Vince's. It was his responsibility to know the age of someone he was having sex with. Though, I doubted asking for ID was going to become popular in the bushes of Lincoln Park.

"You didn't go to prison, though," I said, because it was obvious.

"First offense. I got a suspended sentence, probation and a hefty fine. I think the judge was sympathetic."

"But there's a felony on your record. So your job is at risk."

He nodded. "It's not easy being out in the world of finance. A lot of the people I work with want to get rid of me. If they knew, I'd be gone."

"But they won't find out unless there's a reason to run another check on you."

"Or if someone tells them."

"Rita Lindquist. She's been blackmailing you."

"Yes."

"So, you want me to find away to get rid of her without her exposing you. Is that it?"

"Yes. I've been trying to figure out a way to do it myself, but I couldn't."

"It would have been nice if you'd told me this last month."

"I'm sorry."

"The most obvious way to deal with this is to find out what Appleton is up to and then make a deal with her: You won't prosecute him if they both just disappear. You said you weren't sure if Appleton was inept or criminal. Tell me more about that."

"There were a couple of complaints. From clients. They expected better returns. He may have simply overpromised."

"Or?"

"I don't know. After the clients complained their returns improved. One of them sent in a letter apologizing. Does that fit with what you've found out?"

"All I really know right now is that he lied up a storm on his resume. If I have to guess, I'd guess he's up to something criminal. The lies on his resume weren't stupid. He did go to UCLA; he just didn't finish. So if someone knows UCLA well, he does too. One of the places he says he worked doesn't exist, but he'd probably say they closed that office. And who knows, maybe they did."

"So, we need to figure out exactly what he's up to."

"Yes, we do."

———

THE NEXT MORNING, I got up early and grabbed the *Daily Herald* out of the hallway in front of my door. Margaret Thatcher gave Hong Kong back to the Chinese with the caveat that the city could be capitalist until 2047—a decision that will please or displease a generation not yet born. The Cubs are suing to allow lights at Wrigley field, threatening the Chicago tradition of calling in sick to work and catching a game. And Commonwealth Edition was raising their rates.

Ross was asleep, which I was glad about. He often didn't sleep well. I made coffee and Joseph tip-toed around getting ready to go to FirstChicago. He was just out of the shower when I said, "Oh, shit."

"What?" he whispered.

"I'm awake," Ross said.

"Sorry."

"It's okay. Sounds like something interesting is going on."

"I'm reading 'The Silver Spoon.'"

"Oh, gossip."

"'What cheerleading socialite was seen wobbling around Marshall Field's after hours and hours of drinking those marvelous coffee drinks in the Walnut Room? And which of her paramours was she buying all those ties for? One? Or all?'"

"Is she talking about your friend Sugar?"

"Yes," I said, glumly. If Joseph could figure out who she meant then most of Chicago could.

"Makes her sound like a drunken whore," Ross said. "Well, a drunken whore with a lot of money."

"Yeah, I think that's the point."

Joseph kissed the top of my head and said, "Sorry, Nick. I know you hate it when people are shitty to your friends."

"It's worse than that. Sugar thinks Gloria Silver might have someone following her around. So, on Tuesday I followed her around Field's while she bought ties and gloves. I didn't see anybody, but there was obviously someone watching her."

"You were in Field's on Tuesday?" Joseph asked. "You didn't mention that."

"Yes. Sugar wants me to check out this guy she's fallen for."

"Sounds like you did a lot at Field's."

"Don't get too excited, I haven't got your Christmas present yet," I admitted.

"Don't worry about it. I haven't gotten yours either," he lied.

I was tempted to call him on it but something else occurred to me. "Could you pick up something for Mrs. Harker? Nothing extravagant."

"Um, sure. Are you going there for Christmas?" he asked, ready to be upset.

"No, she's coming here."

"Oh. My goodness." I couldn't tell if that was a good my goodness or a bad my goodness.

And then I told him about our trip to the doctor. I hadn't said anything the night before because, well, mainly because I wasn't ready to talk about it. Also, I'd gotten home just as *Dynasty* started, which we followed with *St. Elsewhere*. I could have fit Mrs. Harker's story in during the commercial breaks, but I didn't think that was right. And then it was time for bed and I was tired and still not ready to talk about it.

"That's terrible," Joseph said. "Do you think she'll be okay coming to dinner?"

"I have no idea." Probably not was a better answer, but I decided to be vague. No use both of us stressing out about it. "I'd better call Sugar."

As I dialed, I couldn't help thinking this had thrown a real wrench into my day. I'd hoped to spend the day figuring out exactly what a financial planner did so I could better understand what Bill Appleton might be up to. I could do it on Friday, but I had to take Mrs. Harker for X-rays smack dab in the middle of the day, which meant I wouldn't really get much done.

I got a busy signal. But I shouldn't have. I was sure Sugar had Call Waiting. She could certainly afford the extra charge. I was pretty sure a busy signal meant there was already a call waiting. That meant she was being swamped with calls about the mention in "The Silver Spoon."

Poor Sugar. I needed to get down there. I negotiated with Joseph to let me take a quick shower before he started getting ready for work. As soon as I was done, I threw on a pair of jeans, a T-shirt, a big black cotton sweater, my trench coat and I was out the door.

It was cold, dark and cloudy, but it wasn't raining. Or snowing. Still, my hair was wet and that alone sent a chill down my spine. Sugar lived in the Gold Coast on East Cedar, a block or two north of Oak. There was also an Elm and a Maple down there. I think I remember her saying once it was like living in a very expensive forest. I could have taken the express bus, but that meant standing around while my hair froze. I gave in and hailed a cab.

Sugar lived in an ornate, three-story brownstone squeezed between two high-rises. The front door was up twelve steps. The basement popped halfway out of the ground and I suppose it was more accurate to say that the house had four floors. I rang the doorbell. A few moments later, Sugar came out to the foyer. She still looked like a teenager. Her blond hair was soft, natural-looking—though it was probably dyed—and pulled back into a pony tail. She wore a men's pink dress shirt and a dark pair of blue jeans. She was barefoot.

She was carrying her beige desk phone. It had the longest cord I'd ever seen and it wouldn't surprise me to find out Illinois Bell had made it special for her.

"Yes, Margret, believe it or not I actually do try to stay out of the newspaper." She listened, and waved me in. "Well short of putting a hit on Gloria Silver I don't know what to do. Honestly, I was completely sober, Christmas shopping and minding my own—" Obviously she'd been interrupted. She was forced to listen. "You know that Gloria embellishes the truth. When she isn't outright making things up, that is. Listen, darling, there's someone here. I have to go."

She stopped to listen again and it was obviously not good-bye she was listening to. "All right, we'll talk later."

She hung up without waiting for Margret to say goodbye.

I raised a questioning eyebrow at her. So she said, Margret Pilson, my former sister-in-law."

"Sugar, I'm so sorry."

"Don't be. Gloria has spies everywhere. It might have been one of the sales clerks. In fact, it probably was."

I wasn't convinced. I'm sure Gloria had lots of spies but doubted that she had one on every floor of Marshall Field's. The phone began to ring again. Sugar ignored it.

"I still feel like I screwed up."

"It won't make any difference. People want me to write checks, so they'll still invite me everywhere. Now they'll just be surprised when I show up sober and fail to make a pass at their husbands. Have you had breakfast?"

"No. I came straight here."

She punched one of the clear buttons on the phone, dialed a single number and a moment later said, "Gretchen, could you get Mr. Nowak some breakfast. Anything in particular, Nick?"

"I'm not picky."

"Whatever you can find is fine, Gretchen. Oh, and could you set up coffee in the dining room."

The living room was wonderfully decorated in shimmering blues. There were two sofas and behind one a French provincial desk. She hung up and set the phone on the desk.

"So, Gloria has it out for you because you stole her boyfriend. Do you think that's the only reason?"

"She didn't like me very much before."

'Why not?"

"I don't know. You can ask her tonight if you like. Though I imagine she'll deny it."

"Tonight?"

"Yes, she's coming to the open house."

"You invited her?"

"The whole point of an open house is the publicity."

"The *Daily Herald* is not the only newspaper in town." Though it was usually the one I read.

"The other papers have also been asked."

"It's not going to make for a pleasant evening with Gloria there."

"No. But it will make for an interesting one." She smiled deviously enough that I wondered if she had something up her sleeve.

We went into the dining room and found that a coffee tray had already magically appeared. Sugar poured for us both. I hadn't done much on Michael Frank, so I changed the subject.

"Do you have a financial planner?" I asked.

"No, darling, financial planners are for people who have enough money to think they're rich but aren't. Why are you asking me that?"

"It's for another case. I have to figure out what a financial planner does so I can figure out what one might do wrong."

"Well, that sounds interesting."

"So, how do you take care of your money?" I asked. It was simple nosiness and had nothing to do with the Renaldi case.

"Myself. Occasionally I ask my ex-husband, Angus, for advice."

"Oh. I didn't know you were on good terms."

"Shhhh, it's a secret. We don't like people to know."

"Really, why?"

"That's one of the tricks of public life. It doesn't really matter what people think about you as long as it's not the truth. If everyone knows the truth, then everyone knows you. The fact that people think I'm a gold digging hussy actually affords me a tiny bit of privacy."

"And that's why you're not very upset about the things Gloria writes?"

"Well, no, she is upsetting me. There's meanness behind what she's doing. She's not just saying silly things about me to grab attention. She's trying to hurt me."

"So, what is the truth about your marriage to Angus Pilson?"

She sighed. "I do miss the South. In the South a gentleman would never ask a lady to tell the truth."

Gretchen, a sturdy, dour woman, came in with a breakfast plate for me. It was full to the edges with scrambled eggs, hash browns, bacon *and* sausage, and thick, homemade toast.

"Gretchen, that looks lovely," Sugar said.

"Yes, thank you."

"Would you like some, Sugar?" Gretchen asked.

"Oh goodness no. One breakfast is plenty."

From the look on Gretchen's face, my guess was Sugar's breakfast hadn't amounted to much. When she left, Sugar said, "I have an idea."

I couldn't respond since I'd already crammed some hash brown potatoes into my mouth.

Sugar continued, "What if we go see a financial planner? That way you could get a really good idea of what they do."

"How do we avoid giving them any money?"

"We could pretend to be newlyweds unsure about what we should do with the million-dollar check Daddy gave us at the wedding, so we're shopping around trying to figure out who has the best advice. There's a place in the Hancock next to Bonwit Teller; we could go there."

I swallowed. "All right. Sure."

"I'll call for the car."

"Sugar, it's three blocks."

"It's five. And it's frigid out there. I'll order the car for ten minutes." And with that, she left the room. I chewed on some bacon and wondered what I was getting into.

Approximately, thirteen minutes later, Sugar's driver was letting us out in front of the Hancock. I may have still had egg in my mustache. The plaza in front of the tower was crowded with people, most of them carrying shopping bags, going every which way. Water Tower Place was next-door, boasting Lord & Taylor and Field's. Neiman Marcus was a block down and I. Magnin across the street. Not to mention the dozens of other stores within spitting distance, as they say.

There was a Salvation Army Santa standing next to the front entrance. Sugar grabbed me by the arm and said, "Let's go through Bonwit's."

"Are you afraid of Santa Claus?"

"No. Gloria's spies. If I walk by the Santa I'm a cheap-skate. If I throw in some spare change I'm still a cheapskate. But if I toss in a wad of cash or write a check, then I'm lording my wealth over ordinary Chicagoans. There's no way for me to win."

"I guess I should be glad I'm broke."

"Don't be insane, it's always better to be rich."

We walked through Bonwit's until we were in the lobby of the Hancock. Sugar looked around for a moment and said, "There."

Lombardi/Smith had a small space next to Bonwit Teller. Well, actually it fronted on the lobby, but did not go all the way through to the street so it was more surrounded by Bonwit's than next to it. The tasteful sign in the window told you nothing about their business.

Sugar tucked a furry white arm into mine and marched me over. As soon as we stepped into the investment firm, a hush fell over us. A young girl sat behind a broad desk. When she looked up she nearly whispered, "Who would you like to see?"

"Oh it doesn't matter, whoever's available," Sugar shrugged.

The girl looked at us suspiciously and said, "One moment." Then got up and walked away. *Didn't they have an intercom system?* I wondered. Either they didn't or the girl didn't know how to use it. Sugar looked at me with a smirk on her face. Oh, God. This was going to be interesting.

Somewhere Christmas-themed Musak played. I think it was "I'll Be Home for Christmas," but it was almost too bland to recognize. The girl came back and said, "John Flough will see you." It sounded like the girl had said, "Flawff."

Sugar raised an eyebrow as if to say, "Flough?"

We thought the girl might lead us to his office, but when she realized we weren't moving she said, "Two doors down on the right."

"Okay."

We walked two doors down and poked our heads in on John Flough. He was model-handsome, with close-cropped blond hair and blue eyes. He looked as though he did two things in life: go to the gym and sit behind his desk looking vaguely confused.

"Hello, we'd like to talk to you about—" I began.

"You're Sugar Pilson," he said. Apparently, he wasn't as confused as he looked.

"Well, yes, I am," she said.

His smile was enormous and showed most of his teeth. "It's such an honor to meet you," he said.

"Oh my, aren't you the perfect gentleman."

"What can I do for you?"

"Well, my friend here, Nicholas, has a tiny little nest egg he'd like to invest, so we're visiting different firms…"

He had a little trouble keeping that smile on his face when he realized Sugar Pilson wasn't there to talk about Sugar Pilson.

"How tiny are we talking?"

"Five hundred thousand."

"That's a respectable amount," he said, glancing at me. I was not dressed like I had a half a million dollars. Nevertheless, he opened a desk drawer and began bringing out brochures. "Here are several funds we recommend. Each one with a return of more than twelve percent last year."

"That's nineteen-eighty three," Sugar asked.

"Yes, ma'am."

"Well, they won't return that this year. It's been a terrible year in the market."

"Well, things have improved in the fourth quarter."

"Yes, but not that much. Nick, you can get a CD at ten percent with none of the risk."

"One of these is a bond fund with a return of…" he flipped through the prospectus. "Eleven and a half percent."

"And how much do you make if you sell this fund to my friend?"

"We don't disclose that information."

"Of course not."

That was for my benefit. He was making his money from commissions on what he sold.

"So, do the riskier funds have higher commissions?" I asked.

"I can't really—I can assure you that our focus at Lombardi/Smith is the client."

We just smiled at him.

"Have you thought of a real-estate limited partnership? The tax benefits are excellent."

She turned to me and said, "When they mention tax benefits it means you're going to lose money for a very long time. I am morally opposed to losing money even if I can write it off on my taxes."

Weakly, he said, "They're very popular."

"Now, what if I wanted you to pick for me? Do people do that?" I asked.

"Yes, of course, that's a discretionary account. It's what we're here for, really. We would have you fill out a limited power of attorney and then discuss the level of risk you're willing to accept, and then I'll choose which instruments to put you into. From time to time I'll tweak your portfolio to make sure it's returning—"

"What's a *limited* power of attorney?"

"It just relates to your account with us. A full power of attorney would allow us to access your bank account, sell your home, things we don't really want to do. This would be a power of attorney for a specific purpose."

I sat back in the guest chair. I could certainly see that there were a lot of opportunities for abuse, particularly with the limited power of attorney. But how was I to prove that?

"How often do I get statements?" I asked.

"Monthly."

"And who has access to that information?"

"Well, no one."

"Really?"

"I mean, we keep records, obviously. In the computer. So Lombardi/Smith employees, I suppose, but only those who actually need—"

"That's a lot of no ones."

He leaned forward. "Well, half the people here don't know how to use the computer anyway.'

I smiled. "That's so reassuring."

"So, can we open you an account?"

"Oh, well, no," Sugar said. "We still have to go to Charles Schwab, Merrill Lynch, and Lehman. We have a full day ahead of us."

"Well, those are all much larger firms than ours. Reputable of course, but I don't know that you'll get the same kind of personalized atten—"

"We'll keep that in mind," Sugar promised. "Such a pleasure to meet you, Mr. Flough."

Chapter Six

BACK IN THE Hancock's lobby, after we stopped giggling about the name "Flough," we looked around for a payphone. When we found it, Sugar called for her car and I called Vincent Renaldi.

"I need to come see you. I have some ideas," I said when he came to the phone.

"We can meet at that restaurant again."

"Listen, I need some information. I think it would be better if I came in."

"Can we do it after the holiday? I'm leaving this after-noon for Springfield—"

"I think we need to do it now," I said.

After a pause, he said, "Tell me what you need."

"I need statements for all of Appleton's clients who've given him a limited power of attorney. And I need copies of the complaints you received and the other letter you mentioned, the one where the client apologized."

He went silent. Then he said, "Let me put you on hold." And he was gone.

I pressed the receiver against my shoulder and said to Sugar, "This is going to take a while. I'll see you tonight."

"You're a doll," she said before planting a wet, sloppy kiss on my cheek. Then she ran off and I went back to listening to a dead line.

Finally, Vincent came back, "Come to the twenty-second floor, conference room A."

And then he hung up on me. Bizarre.

Down in the financial district there was an amazing hundred-year-old building made of cinnamon-colored stone called The Rookery. It was remarkable; the kind of building I could go into and walk around for hours. The glass-ceilinged lobby, the grand wrought iron staircases. Peterson-Palmer was located in the bland, gray thirty-story building across the street.

I was fairly certain the investment firm was located on the fourteenth floor, so it was strange that I was supposed to go to the twenty-second. Before getting on the elevator, I went to the directory and looked up Peterson-Palmer. Next to their name it said 14, 22. So they'd expanded beyond the fourteenth floor. Had HR been moved to twenty-two or was I going to another department? I got onto the elevator and pressed 22. With a muffled whir, we started upward. After a few stops, I was alone when the car arrived at the twenty-second floor.

Getting out of the elevator I immediately noticed that this was the quiet part of the company. From having visited Renaldi on the fourteenth floor in the past, I knew that things down there were pretty noisy.

On the fourteenth floor, there was a traders' area, where the actual traders hung out and kept their things when they weren't on one of the various trading floors or pits. Every afternoon, the traders brought back tickets. Each ticket was divided into different areas where numbers were written by hand. I remember being shown a ticket or two. They didn't make much sense to me. But they did make sense to a bank of data entry clerks, who input the tickets into two rows of CRTs.

Next to the traders were analysts who spent their days digging through stacks of data, prospectuses and computer printouts. Each desk had a computer on which they watched flashing numbers that meant something well beyond my understanding.

That took up half of the fourteenth floor. Another area was devoted to spaces for the financial planners to meet with clients. That was separated from the traders and analysts by a wall of glass. The theory was, having investors watch what actually happened to their money would excite them. And apparently it worked. The final corner of that floor was devoted to the executive offices and HR.

I wasn't sure what that left for the twenty-second floor, but whatever it was it wasn't noisy. I went to my right and followed a sign to conference room A. I walked into the room and found it dark. Running my hand up and down the wall by the door, I found the switch and turned the light on. There was an enormous table surrounded by twelve impor-tant-looking leather chairs. The windows offered a view into a taller, steel-faced building about thirty-feet away. I sat down and made myself comfortable. Having a cigarette would have made me more comfortable, but I didn't see an ashtray and it was rude to stub out a cigarette on carpet. Particularly one as plush as the one they'd chosen.

I'd only been sitting there a couple of minutes, when a young man of about twenty-five walked in humming a tone-less version of "Jingle Bells" and carrying a stack of papers. As soon as he saw me he stopped and said, "Well, hello there."

I didn't know his name, but I figured it was some version of Trouble. I said, "Hey."

He sat down, not taking his eyes off me. "Are you waiting for Vincent Renaldi?"

"Yes."

"I like Vincent. He's kind of humpy, don't you think?"

Vincent was humpy, but I didn't see the point in agreeing. After a few more excruciating minutes, Renaldi walked in. "Sorry I'm late. Did you two meet?"

"Not exactly," I said.

"Oh, well, this is Raymond Dewkes. He's in the MIS department."

"I nodded."

"Raymond, this is Nick Nowak. He's a private investigator who's been doing our background checks for years."

"I thought that's what Rita did?"

Vincent paled. Obviously, he hadn't thought Rita made her way up to the twenty-second floor. "How do you know Rita?"

"She brought cookies up. A couple of times."

"Did she ask for information?" I asked before Vincent could.

"She wanted to know how things worked. What kind of reports we could run and who could ask for them."

"And you told her?"

"She wasn't asking me. It was Jim Tinker she was talking to. Well, shoving her boobs in his face and asking questions. Bill told her everything she wanted to know. I wouldn't have given her the time of day."

"Does anyone know you ran these reports for me?" Vincent asked.

"No. Though I'm supposed to write down everything I do and give it to Jim. And Jim still could find out I ran it if he looked in the print queue."

"And then Jim would tell Rita," I said.

"Does Jim look in the print queue?" Vincent asked.

Raymond looked from me to Vincent, then said, "I'm getting the impression you don't want Rita to know about this."

"No, we don't," Vincent said. "And we don't want her to know about Nick, either."

"You want me to go into the print queue and delete the job."

"Could you?" Vincent asked.

"Yeah, I guess." He smiled at Vincent in an obviously flirtatious way. Vincent seemed not to pick up on it.

"Good." Vincent turned to me and said, "Here are the letters we talked about." He handed me a thin manila file. He glanced at Raymond, who took the hint and slid the stack of papers over to me.

"These are all of Appleton's clients who gave him a limited power of attorney?" I asked.

"The discretionary accounts, yes. There are fifteen of them. Those are statements going back three months."

I glanced at Vincent, I wasn't sure three months was enough, but sending Raymond back to get more right now didn't seem like a good idea. I picked up the statements and glanced at the one on top. There were a lot of abbreviations and fractional numbers. It looked as easy to read as hieroglyphics.

I glanced up at Raymond and asked, "Do I get a decoder ring?"

He smiled at my joke. He had a very nice smile. A few years ago I would have him bent over the table in five minutes. Standing up, I looked at Vincent and said, "Let me talk to you a minute." Then to Raymond I asked, "Can you wait here?"

The boy shrugged.

In the hallway, I closed the door to the conference room.

"What is it?" Vincent asked. "Is there a problem?"

"Raymond thinks you're humpy."

"Is this high school?"

"You need to go back in there and fuck him."

"You do realize I fire people for doing exactly that."

"You also fire people for concealing felony convictions."

"You really think I should?"

"Do you want him on your side?"

"He's kind of already on my side, though. That's why I asked him to—

"More on your side," I said.

He got a grim look on his face. "Okay. Point taken."

Still, he didn't go back into the room. Instead he bit his lip and frowned.

"Don't look so glum. He's young, attractive and willing. You can't ask for much more in a man."

––––––––

I WALKED up to the French Bakery and had lunch at the bar. A roast beef au jus on French bread. It had looked good the other day when Vincent ordered it. I took a quick glance through the statements and felt my stomach sink. It was page after page of abbreviated fund names and long numbers with decimal points. It didn't make a lot of sense to me and I was going to have to struggle with it until it did.

The thing I didn't find, which I'd been hoping to find, was withdrawals. Cash moving out of the accounts in strange ways. Appleton had a power of attorney on these accounts so he could just move money out whenever he felt like it. There were withdrawals, of course, but they didn't seem out of the ordinary. A few hundred here and a thousand there. Obviously, the people who owned the accounts would need some of their money now and then. None of it seemed out of the ordinary.

This would have been much easier if he'd just moved fifty thousand out of each account on a monthly basis. See, that would be unusual. But there was nothing like that, nothing obvious. I did notice quickly that the overall value of the accounts was decreasing at a significant rate. But then, the stock market had been in a slide for the first half of the year. Things had corrected since August, though, and I was looking at statements for September, October, November. Would those months still be reflecting the dip in the first half of the year? Or would they track the market? Was it possible that Appleton wasn't doing anything wrong? Or was it just hard to see? Given my relative inexperience in the world of finance I decided to go with the latter.

My sandwich came and I washed it down with a cold beer. The abbreviations on the statements were fund names. I knew that much. Things like V DIVI, which probably meant Vanity Dividend Fund or some such. I was going to have to sit down and make a chart to see which, if any, of the funds appeared in all the accounts. I could at least figure out if he was aggressively buying funds that paid a higher commission. But that would have to wait until I got back to my office.

I was finishing up the pommes frites that came with my sandwich, when I decided to look at the complaints to see if they told me anything. Vincent had given me three letters from two clients, the two complaints and the one follow-up apology. I decided to start with the client who reversed herself. Her name was Naomi Bellingham. The first letter she'd sent in was written in an unstable cursive.

"I showed my statement to a dear friend and she said it's wrong, I should not be losing money. I should be making money. Why am I not making money? That's what I want to know?"

The second letter was typed. It said,

"I am very happy with the work Bill Appleton has done

for me. He's such a kind young man. I know I worried that I wasn't making any money, but my account seems to have recovered. I understand that financial returns fluctuate. Thank you."

It was signed in the same craggy hand as the first letter.

I flipped through and found Naomi's statements for the last three months. I glanced at the total value of her accounts. In September she had $623,574.22. In October, $630,211.15. And, in November $638,752.92. More than $15,000 in two months. Wait, no, more. Naomi withdrew $1,200 each month to live on. So, nearly $18,000. Roughly a three percent return in three months. One percent each month. That seemed like a lot. Those kinds of returns made Bill Appleton a financial genius.

Of course, Naomi's losses went back further, so I couldn't see how much she lost. My guess was she'd lost much more than $18,000. The gains were to mollify her. But that didn't make sense. Appleton couldn't just manipulate fund prices just to suit him. Could he?

I turned my attention to the other letter, which was written out carefully in block letters. It looked more like a grocery list than a letter. It read,

Dear Sirs,

My father, Paul Johnstone, was a client of yours up to his recent death. He worked with your financial planner, Bill Appleton. In going over my father's monthly statements I've noticed some significant problems. Problems that, over time, have caused staggering losses to his wealth. I would like to come in and discuss with Mr. Appleton's superior what can be done about this.

Thank you,

Edward Johnstone

The letter had been sent on Johnstone's business stationary. A bakery on Lincoln Avenue just west of Boystown.

The bartender, Lu, brought over my check and asked in her gravel-strewn voice, "Are you coming to my party Saturday?"

I didn't actually know she was having a party, but said, "Oh yeah, looking forward to it." Brian was probably supposed to invite me and forgot or had told me and I forgot. Either way, I doubted I was going.

I paid the bill, left a big tip to make up for lying about the party and left. I took the Jackson Howard to Fullerton and then changed to the Ravenswood. I got off at Paulina. My best guess was that Edward Johnstone's bakery was near that stop. It was a good guess, since I found it two storefronts down from the Paulina station.

The bakery was called The Flour Shop, which was supposed to be funny I guess. I walked in and there was a big display case a few feet from the door. It was filled with baked goods: muffins, breads, cookies, cakes, pies. Apparently, Edward did it all. The case and the baking area behind it took up one storefront. A second storefront had been added on and filled with café tables and bentwood chairs. There were five or six people in there drinking coffee and eating pastries. Behind the counter was a tubby guy of about forty wearing an apron.

"I'm looking for Edward Johnstone?"

"Yeah? Who are you?"

"I'm Nick Nowak. I'm working with Peterson-Palmer—"

"Fuck you. Get out of my store."

"I take it you're Edward Johnstone? I'm here about the letter—"

"Yeah I know why you're here and I said get out."

"Okay, tell me what happened. Tell me why you're so mad."

His mouth dropped open. Apparently, simply saying

Peterson-Palmer meant I should know. "You guys sent that awful woman around to threaten me."

"Tell me about her."

He stopped, looked me up and down, decided to trust me, at least a little, and said, "Take a seat. I'll bring you some coffee."

I picked out the table furthest away from his other customers. If he got surly with me again, I didn't want it damaging his business. A couple minutes later, he brought over a gigantic cup and saucer filled with coffee, and a plate with two enormous muffins: one cranberry orange and the other cinnamon. He sat down across from me while I took a sip of the coffee. It was good.

"I have three years of my father's statements from Peterson-Palmer. The first year looks pretty normal. My father made an eight percent return. You can get more from a simple CD right now, but it's still respectable. Then Bill Appleton took over my father's account."

"Why didn't your father handle his own account?"

"Senility."

"I'm sorry."

"Don't be. In some respects it made him a nicer person."

"You didn't get along. Is that why he gave Appleton the power of attorney?"

"Yes. A very expensive decision as it turns out."

"Tell me what happened after Appleton took over your father's account."

"I wish I had the statements so I could walk you through it."

"Give it a try anyway," I said. Having seen the statements, I didn't think they'd be that helpful, anyway.

"Well, I began by tracking each fund through the last two years. Most of them behaved normally, except for three. Appleton bought nearly five thousand shares of Williams

High-Yield II in February of eighty-three. For a couple of months the value grew fractionally and then the fund took a steep dive, losing my father nearly two hundred thousand. It recouped about twenty thousand the next month, then it was sold and Appleton bought Hanover Offshore. That fund had slight increases for five months then suffered the same kind of drop as Williams High-Yield II, this time losing almost three hundred thousand on top of the approximately one seventy-five still not recouped from the first dive. The fund bounced back regaining fifty thousand of the lost money, but then again, Appleton sold the fund and moved the money into someone called Asylum Futures. Two months later, my father died and activity on the account stopped."

"And Asylum Futures made a drop shortly after your father's death?"

"I don't know. That part was challenging. You see, none of the funds are listed."

"So they don't exist?"

"They're not listed on the big exchanges. You can find them if you go to the pink sheets."

"What are the pink sheets?"

"Honestly, I'm not all that sure. By the time I got that deep into it I was way over my head. The only thing I really understand is that my father lost over four hundred thousand dollars in a very short time."

I multiplied that amount over all the accounts I had statements for and it added up to a really significant amount of money.

"Okay, this sounds pretty bad. You're sure Appleton isn't just bad at picking mutual funds."

"Williams High-Yield II, Hanover Offshore and Asylum Futures are all funds managed by the same company. Williams Hanover Management."

"So, the only bad funds he picks come from this same company."

"Yes."

"Have you done anything other than complain to Peterson-Palmer?"

"That's a little tricky. My father's estate is in probate. Legally I'm not supposed to know anything about his accounts."

"How did you get the statements?"

"My father was hospitalized for the last few weeks of his life. I visited his home several times during that period."

"That doesn't sound inappro—"

He shook his head. "I nearly got arrested for burglary."

"You're not in the will," I guessed.

"No. The money goes to a charity, Best Buddies, I think. Something like that. I haven't been able to get much information. They won't even give me a copy of the will."

"And the executor of the will is?"

"Bill Appleton."

Chapter Seven

MICHAEL FRANCE LIVED in a house with a white picket fence, a white clapboard house of a story and a half that looked like it had been teleported in from New England. It sat on the corner of Webster and Racine, and was remarkable in that it had somehow survived decades of red brick townhouses and duplexes being built all around it. Next to the house, and almost as large, was a building that had likely begun as a carriage house, been converted to a garage at some point, and was now an artist's studio. The two buildings were attached by a rather wide breezeway.

When Brian and I walked into the studio, Michael France was posed on the far side of the large room as though waiting to be sketched. He wore a pressed white shirt, festive green and red suspenders, a pair of cuffed rayon pants with a pleated front, and a heavy pair of black oxfords. His hair was slicked back, except for one strand that had artfully escaped.

He, and the party, had a distinctly fifties feel. It felt as though he'd decided the eighties were simply not elegant and had reverted to a time that was. Peggy Lee was warbling some Christmas songs through a rather expensive stereo system. A waiter passed straight-up martinis and manhattans in tall, thin-stemmed glasses. There was an aluminum Christmas tree in one corner decorated with red ornaments.

As we hung our coats on a coatrack set up by the door, Sugar floated over in a stunning red satin dress. It, too, was straight out of the fifties with its skintight bodice and enormous skirt sticking nearly straight out due to all the stiff petticoats beneath. She had a martini in one hand and a bit of mistletoe in the other.

"There you are!" Sugar squealed when she saw us. "Michael! Michael, come meet Brian and Nick."

She held up the mistletoe and kissed me and Brian on our cheeks, enveloping us in a cloud of very expensive perfume. Then she stepped back.

"Well, look at me. A drink in one hand and mistletoe in the other. When that bitch calls me a drunken slut in the newspaper I will have lived up to it."

I glanced around the room to make sure the bitch wasn't already there. She didn't seem to be. There were a dozen people scattered around the studio looking at the two gigantic paintings set up on large easels: one an orchid, the other a flamingo. They all looked well-to-do, dressed in expensive clothes, but it was more than that. Naked, these people would look rich. The face creams and hairdressers and spa treatments and expensive exercise classes and a hundred other little details that all cost money, all left their mark.

"Michael, this is Nick Nowak and Brian Pearson. My friends." I figured she'd already had at least two martinis since the loose Texas vowels were coming out.

Holding out a hand, Michael France said, "Hello. Thank you for coming." His vowels were clipped and very East Coast. Maybe too East Coast. "Sugar has said so many kind things about you both."

"Nice to meet you," I said.

"She's said really, really nice things about you, too. She talks about you *all* the time. I feel like I know you. Inside out," Brian said, then seemed to regret it. He'd made it sound like she'd said too much. And she probably had.

"And a Merry Christmas to you both," Michael France added.

We all Merry Christmas-ed each other. The waiter came by with drinks and we emptied his tray.

"It's an interesting house," I said.

"It is. It's quite old. There aren't many wooden houses in Chicago and few this old. The house predates the Chicago Fire."

"And so does the plumbing," Sugar added.

France cleared his throat. "Yes, the fire stopped a few blocks from here."

"Close call," I said.

"Webster Avenue used to be called Asylum Place. There was an insane asylum on this spot before they built the house."

"Really? That's fascinating," Brian said.

"That's a lot of local history for someone from...New York?"

He laughed. "I had an excellent real-estate agent. Excuse me, I have more guests."

Luckily for him, some new people had walked into the studio. An older gentleman and his recently purchased second wife. The poor girl looked incredibly nervous. I imagined her having a bad case of second wife-itis. A disorder that kept her focused on increasing her social standing by wearing the right clothes, helping the right charities, going to the right parties, buying the right art. All in an attempt to distract from the fact that she was screwing an old man for money.

I wondered if Sugar had suffered from the same disorder

during her brief marriage to Angus Pilson. As if to answer me, she said, "I'd better go over there. I need to hide that poor girl in a corner before Gloria gets here. You boys mingle, I'll be back later."

And then she was gone. Brian and I looked at each other.

"This isn't really my crowd," he said.

"Mine either. But I'm not here to mingle anyway. Let's go stand over there," I said, pointing at a spot in front of the giant orchid painting. I wanted to get a better look at it.

The painting was probably six foot by eight foot. I had no idea what kind of an orchid it was. The petals where magenta and white and looked something like a diagram of the human circulatory system. At the center of each bloom there were a couple of almost-red petals trying to come together like a malformed heart.

"It looks like a photograph," Brian said.

"It does. The way it goes in and out of focus." It was obviously painted from a photograph. If it were painted from life, then the whole painting would be in focus. But instead, the background was a fuzzy gray and one or two of the blooms in the back were hazy. It was an interesting choice. Most of us wouldn't realize that it was a painting of a flower through a camera's eye. But that's what it was. Our eyes didn't blur things in exactly that way.

"It's so real," Brian said. And he was right. If you were talking about the photograph it was copied from. But if you were talking about the painting, well, it just wasn't. The painting was only as real as the photograph allowed.

The Peggy Lee album ended and France put on *Ella Wishes You a Swinging Christmas*. I wanted to stop him. The album was two decades old and should be saved and not played. They'd put it out on cassette a couple years ago, that's what we should be listening to. Who cares what happens to a cassette, right? It just seemed decadent to listen to the actual album. But it was lovely hearing her begin to sing "Jingle Bells."

"Why isn't Franklin here?" I asked Brian.

"His office party is tonight."

"How convenient," I said. I didn't think Franklin was out at work, so he wouldn't have been bringing Brian.

Brian gave me an admonishing glance and said, "I need to spend some time with Ross. I'm not sure when, though. Lu is having a party Saturday—I think I was supposed to invite you to that. Then we have Franklin's friends on Christmas Eve and his family on Christmas Day. So I have to come by either tomorrow night or Sunday."

"Well, he'll be there. I should give you a heads up on something else, though," I said. "Something is going on with Mrs. Harker. You might need to take Terry for a while."

"Something's going on? What does that mean?"

"She's having some stomach pain. The doctor ordered some tests."

"Oh God, I hope she's all right. How old is she?"

"I don't know. Harker would be forty-seven so I'd guess between seventy-five and eighty."

"I hate that people die. It would be so much nicer if we stuck around until we got good and bored and just decided...to leave. I'd rather go to going-away parties than funerals."

Fitzgerald was part way through "Have Yourself a Merry Little Christmas" when Gloria Silver arrived wearing a mink coat as large and as black as a bear. She'd allowed the coat to slip over one shoulder so we got a preview of her tailored, silver suit even before she wiggled out of the coat. Her suit was stunning. Made of some kind of artfully crushed silver lamé, it was relatively simple: a short matador-style jacket, a straight skirt with a cobalt blue shell underneath the jacket.

As soon as she got the coat off she made for Michael

France, practically stepping on Sugar to get to him. I said, "Excuse me," to Brian and moved closer.

"It's fabulous. Simply fabulous," Gloria exclaimed.

"You remember Sugar Pilson," he said, since she was being ignored. Of course, Gloria and Sugar met a hundred times a year.

"Why, yes, I do. Who could forget Sugar, try as we might?" With a stiff smile she turned back to France. "Any sales yet?"

"That's not really how this works Gloria, I've explained that before. I don't have anything for sale right now. I'm only taking commissions."

"Well, any of those?"

"No. But it doesn't matter. I have commissions straight through next Christmas."

"Then why on earth are you doing this?" she asked, snatching a drink off a tray.

"It's a way of thanking my clients for their support."

"Oh that's charming. I'll put that in my column."

Just then the nervous second wife bustled over and said, "Mrs. Silver, I'm Joley McMillian. It's such an honor to meet you."

"It is, isn't it?" Gloria replied. She studied the girl with sharp eyes, deciding whether she would support the girl or skewer her. Having read her column, my guess was skewer. Gloria had little love for second wives.

"Joley, you need another drink," Sugar said. "Let's go find a waiter."

"Not so fast," Gloria said. "I have to find out more about this charming young lady." She slipped her arm around the girl and walked her away. "Michael! Never let ladies wander around unescorted."

Dutifully he followed. I looked at Sugar and said, "That was nice of you."

"Why, whatever do you mean?"

"You knew if it looked like you were taking the girl under your wing, Gloria would want to steal her away."

"You didn't talk to that poor, misguided child. Gloria will be sorry. I certainly didn't do her any favors."

"I'm going to try to focus on your case tomorrow," I said, since I hadn't really done much of anything, yet.

"It's all right, darling. I just need to know before I marry him."

"Um, okay, when are you planning to marry him?"

"Well, New Year's Eve would be terribly romantic, don't you think?"

"Sugar, are you sure?"

"Oh, yes, just about anything you do on New Year's Eve is romantic."

"I meant about France."

"Well, provided you don't discover he's a vampire or some such drivel, yes. I mean, look at him. He's gorgeous. And he makes his own pocket money. So I'll never have to give him an allowance. And he makes me happy."

"How much of his success is because of Gloria? He's certainly moved up quickly."

"Gloria got what she paid for," Sugar said, sweetly. "It was always a rental, never a purchase."

Straight people had such an odd way of thinking about things sometimes. They thought casual sex—with its simple exchange of pleasure for pleasure—immoral. But exchanging that same pleasure for a lifetime of comfort was the height of morality.

Brian joined us just then and asked Sugar if there was anyone who might be useful at Howard Brown. She frowned and looked around the room. "Well, I'm sure Joley is in need of a charity. And becoming involved with something like

Howard Brown might have the added benefit of putting her husband in an early grave."

"Should we talk to her about it?"

"Yes, let's see if we can pry her back from Gloria."

They wandered off and I noticed Michael France standing alone near the flamingo painting, so I headed in that direction.

"So, how do you do it?" I asked him. It seemed like a reasonable question to ask a painter. "What's the process?"

"Do you see that wall?" He pointed at the wall that was probably also the end of his property. It was a large empty space.

"Yeah," I said.

"Do you see the counter over there?"

"Yes." I hoped he wasn't going to point out anything else. I was already getting bored.

"Well, I put a projector on the counter and then hang my blank canvas on the wall. I project a slide onto the canvas then I basically trace the image onto the canvas."

"That doesn't sound especially difficult," I said.

"It's not."

"What's the next step?"

"I color in the picture."

"That doesn't sound—"

"Especially difficult? It's not."

"Why flamingos? Why orchids?"

"One of my instructors said that good artists steal from better artists. Can you imagine a better artist than Mother Nature?"

"So why doesn't everyone do it?"

"Because they can't. Something happens while I'm coloring. I don't really understand it, I just do it."

"What would happen if I tried?"

"Unless you, too, are very rare, you'll get a big pink blob."

"Instead of a living, breathing flamingo."

"Yes."

Then everything stopped because Sugar had begun to laugh—a high, angry, mean laugh. "Go ahead, taste it," she said loudly. "Taste it. It's water you stupid bitch. Yes, you'll put it into your column that I was drunk as a skunk. But it's water. W. A. T. E. R. Water. And I'll let you in on another little surprise. I'm only fucking one man in this room."

"Excuse me," France said and rushed across the room. "Sugar, dear."

I took a few steps closer to the action to see what Gloria was going to do. She wasn't cowering or simpering, she just stood there stone-faced and a bit red around the jowls. She turned and walked over to the coatrack and grabbed her fur coat.

France was already leading Sugar away, I was about to join them when Gloria grabbed me by the forearm. I looked down at her talon-like hand and asked, "What do you think you're doing?"

"I could do things for you, you know. If you weren't so close to certain people."

"I don't really need things done for me."

"Everyone needs publicity."

I almost said I didn't, that I actually hated it, which would probably have gotten me a mention in her column every day for a week. "Thanks, I'll keep that in mind." I tried to pull away but she clutched my arm even tighter.

"Has she told you yet?"

"Who? What?"

"Sugar. She has a secret, has she told you? It has to do with her money. Did you ever ask yourself why she has so much of it? A one-year marriage and she ends up with, what? Ten million? Twenty? That's not normal."

She was right, of course, I had wondered about that before. Sugar's life didn't make a lot of sense, so there very likely was a secret at the bottom of it. One that Gloria seemed to know.

"Why play coy, Gloria? You want to tell me. So tell me."

"I'm not saying anything. Not yet."

She tried to walk away but it was my turn to grab her by the wrist. "I don't like people who hurt my friends. If you try to hurt Sugar I'll find a way to hurt you."

She smiled at me. "You're not smart enough," she said as she walked away.

I stood there a moment, hoping she was wrong, hoping I was smart enough to carry through on my threat if I needed to. It kind of sucked that I didn't feel so smart at that particular moment having missed whoever was following Sugar the other day. *Well,* I thought, *if I wasn't smart enough I was going to have to get smart enough.*

Chapter Eight

I WOKE up to Bing Crosby singing a Hawaiian Christmas song. It was far too early and I'd stayed up far too late. The open house had turned into a drinking party and I'd stayed for all of it. I'd thought Sugar had been drinking before, but maybe I was wrong, maybe she was as sober as she claimed. Once Gloria left, though, Sugar tied one on. She was happy and wanted to celebrate.

As it happened, there was no other actual press there during the spat. They arrived a bit later and got an earful about what had happened. Gloria would very likely run an item about Sugar being drunk and slutty, while the other papers would run items about Sugar confronting Gloria about saying she was drunk and slutty. Sugar was likely to come out of the whole thing looking good.

Sleepy-eyed, I went out into the living room and glared at Joseph. He was already dressed for work and busy making French toast. Ross sat on the edge of the pullout looking not much more awake than I was.

"Well?" I asked. "How did it go?"

Joseph gave me a sheepish look. "I only got through part.

They know I've left the priesthood. Honestly, they couldn't take much more and neither could I."

"All right, that's step one, I guess. Why do they think you left the priesthood?"

"Crisis of faith. Which is true."

It just wasn't the whole story.

"Where do they think you live?"

"I told them I have two roommates."

I didn't know how to feel about this. Coming out had not been easy for me. I'd made a number of despicable decisions at the time, so I couldn't exactly criticize. At the same time, I wasn't excited by the way my lover managed to lie and tell the truth at the same time. Did he do that to me?

"What are we listening to?"

"Bing Crosby. I grew up with this. My mom wanted me to have it."

"Does she think a few choruses of 'Silent Night' will bring you back into the fold?"

"That's probably exactly what she thinks," Joseph said.

"And they know you're not coming for Christmas dinner?"

"That's not a problem. We always have dinner with my mother's sister and her family. It's an enormous affair. My not being there means they don't have to tell the truth. They'll just say I'm off giving emergency mass. I did say I'd come by on Christmas Eve, though."

"Wait. Is there such a thing as emergency mass?" Ross asked.

"You'd be surprised," said the former priest.

"They won't want to see you do mass on Christmas?" I asked.

"Oh no, my aunt's family is lapsed."

"Just like you."

He frowned at me. It wasn't exactly an accurate description. But why split hairs? He asked, "How was your party?"

"Fabulous," I deadpanned.

"How is Brian?"

"Hung over, I think. We did a lot of drinking."

"You were working, though," Joseph wondered. "Checking out Sugar's fiancé. Sit down. Have your breakfast."

The French toast was good, but what I really wanted was bacon. Well, bacon and a cigarette.

"I liked him. Her painter. He might still be a complete ass, but he was fun, at least. And he was good with her. Didn't get all pissy when she got drunk."

That earned me a sharp look. Certain people occasionally criticized my drinking. Not to mention my smoking.

"So, I won't see you later, will I?" I asked. It was Friday after all. Cheat day. I had no plans for the evening, but I assumed Joseph did.

"I'm going out around eight."

I didn't ask where he was going.

———

AN HOUR and a half later I was scurrying across the plaza at the Daley Center, the collar of my trench coat pulled tight against the icy drizzle. The Recorder of Deeds was across the street in City Hall, a sooty gray building from the turn of the century. It had two addresses: one on LaSalle and one on Clark. The Clark side held most of what I needed and I spent a good deal of my time there filling out forms and paying fees.

I went through the brass revolving door and decided where to go first. The recorder's office. It was on the first floor off the cavernous, mosaic-topped lobby. I filled out the forms

I needed and then wound my way through the roped-off line and waited. I was fifth in line.

While I waited I made a mental map of what I needed to do that day. Working backward, I had to have Mrs. Harker at Illinois Masonic by 3:30 p.m. for X-rays. That meant I had to pick her up by 3 p.m. or a bit before, say 2:45 p.m. to be safe. So I'd need to leave downtown by 2 p.m. I'd driven down to the Loop and paid eight dollars for all-day parking at the cheapest garage I could find. I wouldn't be there all day, but anything over two hours cost more than the eight bucks. I needed the car to get out to Edison Park on time and I'd charge it to Peterson-Palmer anyway.

It was 10:30 a.m. I had at least three and half-hours to take care of everything I needed. Twenty minutes later, I was out in the lobby leaning up against a marble wall—there wasn't a bench in the place—looking at a copy of the deed for 1179 Webster Avenue. The property belonged to Michael Francelli and Gloria Silver. Obviously there were two big problems with that. One was the name Francelli. Okay, maybe not such a big deal. It was common for artists to rein-vent themselves under another name. It was also common for con artists. The second problem was Gloria Silver. She owned the property with him. I doubted Sugar knew that.

I found an ashtray shoved up against a wall, smoked a cigarette and thought about what to do next. I could run the basics on Michael Francelli—birth, death, marriage—but all that would tell me was whether he'd done any of those things in Cook County.

Since I had a name and address, I could go see a contact I had in the credit department of Carson, Pirie, Scott and sneak a look at his credit report. He probably had great credit since he'd gotten a mort—

Wait a minute. He hadn't gotten a mortgage. There was no trust deed. There was just the regular deed. That meant they'd paid cash. Whose cash? Gloria's? Sugar mentioned that she'd just bought a condo. So, what was the deal with all the real-estate?

What else did I need? I wanted to head over to the main library and check for mentions of Francelli or France in the news. But I didn't want to waste time running back and forth. There were things I wanted to know about Williams Hanover, so I walked the length of the lobby until I got to the other end and the secretary of state's office. Then I went through the same process I'd just gone through, filled out the form, waited in the line, and paid the fee.

Well, almost the same process. Each Certificate of Incorporation sent me to the back of the line. When I was done, I had paperwork on three different corporations: Williams Hanover, Hardy Hastings and Apple Pi Investment Products. Like the funds sold by Williams Hanover, the three corporations were interconnected and meant to swallow one another like Pac-Man. Hardy Hastings was an incorporator of Williams Hanover and Apple-Pi an incorporator of Hardy Hastings. I'd read about shell corporations in the newspaper. I was pretty sure this is what I had in front of me. Entities that were primarily used to pass money back and forth; money that in some way, shape or form wasn't entirely legit. Like, money you were skimming off mutual funds, for instance.

One thing the corporations had in common was their registered agent. Well, their new registered agent. A new sheet was stapled onto the front of each certificate, showing the registered agent to be a woman at 333 West Wacker Drive, Suite #1583, Chicago, IL 60606. I was familiar with the building. They'd been building it most of the time I worked in the Loop, so I'd see it whenever I happened to take an express bus down that way. It had recently opened. Rochelle LaRue became the registered agent for all three corporations on April 10, 1984. Something about the name nagged at me. It sounded familiar, but I couldn't place it. It sounded like a drag name, so that was probably it.

There were other names on the certificates. The original registered agent was Myron Shaver at an address on LaSalle. The other incorporators for all three companies were Walter Seyd and Martin Goewy. I'd have to look them up and see if they were real.

Even though I had copies, I wrote down all the names in the small notebook I carried with me. That way I could dump the papers in my car and still be ready if I needed to look into the names.

I was hungry and should have gone to lunch, but it was nearly one o'clock so I rushed over to the main library. When I got there I decided to start with the easy stuff. There was a bank of phonebooks hanging from dowels right next to the circulation desk. I looked up Rochelle LaRue in the Chicago Metro phone book. She wasn't there.

On a whim, I looked up Rita Lindquist. And as I did, it hit me. R. L. Rita Lindquist and Rochelle LaRue had the same initials. It could have been a coincidence, but my gut said it wasn't. They were the same person. I was sure of it. Rochelle LaRue became the new registered agent after Rita and Bill met. She didn't just fall in love with Bill Appleton, she fell in love with his scam.

In the phonebook I found an R. Lindquist on Pinegrove. Maybe that was her, maybe it wasn't. Women often just used a first initial, so it could be Rebecca or Robin, it didn't have to be Rita. Still, I took down the address and the phone number to check later. I was ready to move on, but then decided to check one more thing. I switched to the yellow pages, which in Chicago was now an entire phone book of its own. I flipped to Private Investigations and found Lindquist Investigations, 333 West Wacker Drive, Suite #1423.

Okay, that sealed it. Rochelle and Rita were definitely the same person. Rita had set it up so that Rochelle's mail came to an address near her, but not to her. Was 1583 an empty office? Or a nonexistent one? If the fourteenth and fifteenth floors were covered by the same mailroom, it wouldn't be hard for Rita to convince a mail boy to bring her Rochelle's mail if and when it showed up.

I doubted Rita was renting two offices in a brand new building. My guess was a law firm occupied those two floors. It wasn't uncommon for a law firm to provide space to an investigator in exchange for services or even just a discount. So maybe Rita bunked in with a law firm that had two floors in the building.

I thought about scanning the legal section of the yellow pages to figure out which law firm was supplying her with an office, but I didn't have that kind of time. I only had about forty-five minutes left.

Turning my attention back to Michael France, I made my way down to the basement and went through the thick indexes for the last five years of the *Daily Herald*, looking for mentions of either Michael Francelli or Michael France. There were two instances of Francelli and twenty-five of France, not including the ones I'd already looked at.

I went to the microfiche desk and asked for the rolls that matched the dates I'd written down. Then I went to the machine and scanned through to find what I wanted. I started with the Francelli mentions.

The first mention I found of Michael Francelli was an article about the Woman's Appreciation for Art handing out scholarships to three students at the Art Institute. Francelli was one of them. The second mention I found was more serious.

"Gallery owner Richard Tamlyn was arrested for

attempting to sell a painting reputed to be by the recently deceased artist Fritz Campion, noted member of the New York School of Abstract Representationalists. Art Institute student Michael Francelli is suspected of creating the fraudulent work."

The article provided a few more details from Campion's life, but they didn't really interest me.

There was more to the story, obviously, but there were no more mentions of Francelli. I could have looked up Tamlyn or Campion to see if the arrest went to trial, but I was running out of time.

Inserting quarters into the fiche machine, I was able to get copies of both Francelli articles. The machine was several years old, so the copies were the hazy, filmy kind you could barely read. They were also my only choice.

I zipped through the twenty-five mentions of Michael France. Most were in "The Silver Spoon." I decided to ignore those and kept speeding through to see if there was anything else. I found a profile of Michael France from two years before. Scanning it quickly, it contained some important biographical information I didn't have. In the article, he was asked, "Where did you study?"

"I don't believe in formal education."

He couldn't tell the reporter he went to the Art Institute since it was easy to check. He couldn't tell the reporter any school he attended for the same reason. He had a good reason not to believe in formal education.

"But you must have gotten some training," the reporter asked.

"I believe in talent. There's no point without it."

Another answer designed to deflect.

"And where were you born? Where did you grow up?"

"A small town in upstate New York."

There were at least five or six hundred of those. Impossible to check.

It was getting late and I didn't have time to read any more. I printed out the article, added it to my little stack, and rushed out of the library. I stepped out into the street, hailed a cab and had him drive me the seven blocks back to the parking garage at Lake and Wells. I gave him a big tip so he didn't hate my guts.

I collected my car and made my way over to the Kennedy, and then took that out to Harlem where I got off and shot into Edison Park. It took about thirty-five minutes, meaning that I was running ten minutes behind. Driving up the Kennedy, I realized I was close to wrapping up both cases.

I knew that France had been involved in some kind of fraud and that he was more involved with Gloria Silver than we'd known. I wondered if there was a way I could find out about the fraud over the weekend; then I could lay it out for Sugar on Monday, Christmas Eve. Okay, so it wouldn't make for a very nice Christmas, but it would probably save her from a worse one later on.

The Peterson-Palmer thing was pretty close to being finished, too. Over the weekend I'd get some graph paper and make a chart of how much money Appleton had stolen from his clients using the sketchy mutual funds. I couldn't connect him to the funds directly, but I could connect Rita. Well, her alter ego. I wondered if there was a way I could connect him, too. It would be a better package if I directly connected him.

I wondered if all of his clients were older. And then I wondered if it was normal to have so many geriatric clients who'd signed a power of attorney.

Something wasn't sitting well with me on either case. But it was okay. I had the weekend to think it through.

I pulled up in front of the Harker condo and there was Mrs. Harker on the curb, waiting. She climbed into the car and scowled at me. I scowled right back.

"Why were you standing on the curb? It's cold and it's raining."

She was wearing a yellow raincoat and a clear plastic rain bonnet, but she still could have waited in the lobby if she was anxious.

"I wait because you late."

"Yeah, I'm sorry about that. I was working. How do you feel?"

"I feel good," she said, then looked away like most liars do.

"Did you take a pain pill?"

"No."

"Did you take one last night?"

"No."

"You're supposed to take them so the pain goes away."

She blew some air through her lips suggesting that was a ridiculous idea.

"Pain is life," she mumbled. And I couldn't argue with her.

The Kennedy had been kind of a mess with the icy rain and all, so I decided we'd be better off taking Elston down to Belmont and cutting over to Boystown. We were quiet most of the way. Too quiet. So I asked, "How's Terry."

"Is good boy."

"Does he come home from school on time?"

She shrugged. "Sometime."

"He needs to come home from school on time all the time."

Another shrug. "Is boy."

I didn't know quite how to explain that Terry probably wasn't up to the things other boys were up to. He wasn't hanging out with boys his age talking baseball scores. And he wasn't sneaking cigarettes in the woods. But then I decided not to bother. It was the wrong time to try to explain to her what kinds of trouble precocious gay teenagers could get up to.

"Thank you. For looking after Terry."

The minute it was out of my mouth I regretted it. Mrs. Harker turned and glared at me like I'd just strung together every swear word I could think of.

It was the timing. I might have been able to get away with it on another day, but we were on our way to see if she was sick—no not *if* she was sick; we were on our way to see how sick she was. And if the speed with which the doctor set up the tests was any indication, she might be very sick. And I'd just said something that was the kind of thing you'd want to sneak in before someone dies. And we both knew it.

Radiology was on the second floor at Illinois Masonic. Once we found it, a bored young nurse studied Mrs. Harker's red, white and blue Medicare card, wrote down her ID number, and then handed it back to Mrs. Harker with a clipboard.

"Can you tell me if the information we have is correct?" She didn't look at us.

Mrs. Harker read the form then handed it back. "Is correct."

The nurse took it, then asked, "Did you take the laxatives as your doctor instructed?"

This was news to me. "What laxatives?"

"Shhhh," Mrs. Harker said. "Yes, I take."

"Your mother is having a barium enema," the nurse said.

I blushed. "She's not my mother."

The nurse seemed to wake up, and looked at me with surprise, then disapproval, as though bringing an old lady for a barium enema was some new kind of perversion.

"You go now," Mrs. Harker said to me.

"What?"

"You go."

"Come back for her in about an hour and a half."

"Can we have a minute?" I asked.

"Take your time. We won't be calling her for at least twenty minutes." She walked away.

"You really want me to leave?"

"Yes."

All I could imagine was her refusing to take off her clothes, or worse, fully understanding what a barium enema was and demanding to leave. I was sure she understood what an enema was. I wasn't so sure she knew the English word for it.

I reached into the pocket of my trench coat and pulled out the bottle of valium Dr. Macht had prescribed. "I have some pills the doctor gave me. They'll make this easier."

"Easy pill? You have easy pill?"

I shook one out into my palm and she looked at it. It didn't take her long to decide. She picked it up and popped it into her mouth. Then she snorted. "Easy pill, ha."

Chapter Nine

I WAS STARVING, so I went right for the cafeteria. I had a hamburger with French fries. The hamburger was only marginally meat and the fries were soggy. I used five packets of ketchup. When I was done, I drank the rest of my pop and smoked a cigarette, flicking the ashes into the dirty paper plate my lunch had been served on.

Mrs. Harker had looked small and defenseless when I walked away. She'd always been such a formidable force that it seemed wrong to see her so diminished. It hadn't been easy being hated by her, but I would welcome that hateful, horrible Mrs. Harker back rather than see her humbled this way.

I had an hour I hadn't planned on. I needed to think up something I could do so that I didn't simply sit there and stew. Knowing I'd have at least a little time, I'd brought my morning's discoveries with me. I read the profile of Michael France again, but there wasn't any point. I doubted much of it was true.

I wanted to—needed to—find out more about Michael Francelli, rather than his invention Michael France. Francelli went to the Art Institute and not that long ago, so someone down there probably knew something about him. But I didn't have time to go there and wander around until I found that someone. Then I had an idea. I went out to the lobby and found a pay phone.

"I can't really talk," I said to Sugar when she came to the phone.

"Do you always start conversations like that? It seems awfully rude."

"Who's the smartest gallery owner in town?"

"Richard Saperstein at Wayne Galleries. It's just off Michigan—"

"Have you bought from him?"

"Yes, several times. I have a Lichtenstein print and—"

"I can use your name?"

"Of course you can. But Nick, it's the holidays. Give yourself a break. I'm sure you'll be able to—"

"Sugar, I have to go," I said, hanging up on her.

Luckily, no one had stolen the phone book that went with the pay phone. I looked up Wayne Galleries and dialed.

"Wayne Galleries," a young woman answered.

"Richard Saperstein, please."

"Can I tell him who's calling?"

"A friend of Sugar Pilson's."

It wasn't exactly a name, so I earned a skeptical "Okay."

A moment later, a man came on the line. "This is Richard. Who is this?"

"Nick Nowak. I'm a friend of—"

"Sugar's, yes, my assistant told me that. Are you interested in purchasing some art?"

"I'm interested in knowledge and Sugar told me you're the smartest gallery owner in town."

He chuckled. "Sugar is one of my favorite clients."

"What can you tell me about Fritz Campion?"

"New York School. Abstract Representationalist."

"What exactly is that? Abstract—"

"It's a school of painting that combines the representational or figurative with the abstract. Larry Rivers' *Dutch Masters* is one of the most famous examples; you may have seen it."

I did know that some painter had gotten famous painting a box of cigars, but I had no memory of the actual painting.

"How much does Campion's work go for?"

"He's been dead about ten years, I'd say his major pieces are going for a hundred thousand. Lesser ones for fifty. Since Rivers and others in the school are still active, the value of a Campion is only likely to go up. I would grab anything you see at fifty or below."

"Provided it's not a fake."

"Ah, that's what you're calling about? The forgery?"

"Yes."

"Well, I don't have any firsthand knowledge of that, of course. Everything I know is gossip."

"Gossip will do."

"Well, Richard Tamlyn was ruined."

"Was he behind the fraud?"

"That's hard to say. The forger was a student out of the Institute. Brilliant copyist. Amazing accuracy. I don't remember the boy's name. I think one of the instructors was involved. He was fired over it at least. So possibly the instructor introduced the boy to Tamlyn and the scheme was hatched."

I decided not to supply the Francelli name. It was so close to France that even an idiot would jump to the truth given my connection to Sugar, and Saperstein didn't seem like an idiot.

"Why did they choose Campion?"

"Several reasons. First, he was active until nineteen

seventy-two when he died. One of the biggest challenges a forger faces is materials. If you're forging a hundred-year-old painting you need a hundred-year-old canvas, and then you have to figure out how to make the oils look as though they've been drying for a hundred years. It doesn't matter how good a copyist you are, the materials can give you way. But a five-year-old painting? Ten? That poses fewer problems."

"I see."

"The other thing about Campion and all of the New York School is that the work itself is challenging to copy. It's audacious even to try."

"So what was their mistake?"

"When you forge a painting you have to decide whether you're going to forge an existing work of art or whether you want to create a new work by a popular artist. In this case, Tamlyn had a lesser Campion which the student copied."

"And then he sold them both?"

"Yes."

"Isn't that risky?"

"Yes, very."

"Why did he think he could get away with it?"

"One went to Ethel Carmichael. You've heard of the Carmichaels?"

"Yes, of course." They were a famous Chicago family on a par with the Pilsons and, if I wasn't mistaken, a family who often married Pilsons.

"The other painting went to a British real-estate developer."

"So Tamlyn thought they'd never cross paths."

"Exactly. But then the Brit went through a nasty divorce and to spite his wife donated the painting to the Tate. Which caused a great deal of publicity. Mainly because of the divorce, not the painting."

"And the story was picked up over here?" I asked. If I'd had more time at the library I would have looked up Campion. And then I would have looked up Tamlyn.

"Yes."

"So who had the forgery? Ethel Carmichael or the Brit?"

"I don't think anyone knows. The experts couldn't agree. The fake was that good."

————

IT WAS ALMOST seven when I walked into my apartment. Mrs. Harker had still been under the effect of the easy pill on the way home and dozed most of the way. When we arrived in Edison Park I roused her and told her I'd see her on Monday when she was having a CAT scan. She simply nodded and got out of the car.

Brian, Franklin and Terry were sitting around my small table, Ross was on the sofa, and Joseph was making a pot of coffee. Brian and Franklin had coffee cups already, so I assumed Joseph was making a second pot. There was a bottle of Kahlua on the table.

Also on the table were the remains of what had been a large plate of holiday cookies. There were only about a dozen left. They were homemade sugar cookies cut in the shape of bells and angels. The bells were dusted with red sprinkles, the angels green. Something about the cookies made me uneasy.

"We were remembering the worst present we ever got," Joseph said. "What's the worst present you ever got, Nick?"

"Did you make these?" I asked Brian.

"God, no," he said.

Ross laughed. He was the cook when they were together. I looked at Franklin and he said, "No, I don't bake. And if I did bake, I wouldn't sprinkle."

"Come on, Nick, worst present?"

"Where did the cookies come from?" I asked him.

"I think my sister left them."

"How does your sister know you live here?"

"Why are you making such a big—I told her I was living by the lake with two roommates." And even as he said it, he knew that she wouldn't have any idea where on the lake. "Well, maybe it wasn't my sister. Maybe it was one of the neighbors."

"As a thank-you for listening to us fuck through the walls?" I asked, crudely. Terry cackled.

"Shush," I told him.

"Or maybe the building management," Joseph suggested weakly.

"How many did you eat?"

"Four, maybe five."

I turned to Ross, "How many did you have?"

"Three."

"Only one," Brian said. "I'm not big on sweets."

"A lot," Terry said, the look on his face suggested he was starting to understand how serious this might be.

"I ate seven. Maybe eight," Franklin said.

The room fell into a very uncomfortable silence.

"Did they taste weird?" I asked. "Was there anything unusual—?"

"They were really good," Terry said.

"Oh God, I've been feeling kind of sick," said Franklin. "I thought it was the Kahlua. That I'd been drinking too—"

He got up and ran to the bathroom. He was puking before he could shut the door and from the splashing sound my bet was he'd missed the toilet entirely.

"Okay, you need to puke, all of you need to puke."

"Nick, you're not being rational," Joseph said. "You probably just scared Franklin, that's all."

"I think I'd better throw up," Ross said. He stood up to

walk over to the kitchen but instead collapsed onto the floor. "Oh shit, I got dizzy."

Brian got down onto the floor with him and started asking if he was all right.

"Okay, we're going to the hospital. Grab everything you need." I looked under the sink and grabbed a few brown paper bags. Into one bag, I put the cookies, plate and all. Then I handed out the other bags.

"What are these for?" Brian asked.

"Airsickness bags. Without flying in the airplane part."

"Oh FUCK!" Terry said, right before he barfed into his bag.

"Do we need an ambulance?" Brian asked.

"I think we'll get there faster if we just drive," I said, though I didn't like the idea of my friends vomiting all over Harker's car. "Come on, let's go."

Brian helped Ross off the floor. I opened the door to the apartment, then stepped over to the bathroom. "Franklin, come on, we're going to the emergency room. When he didn't answer I opened the door. The room reeked. Franklin was on his knees with toilet paper trying to clean up the mess he'd made. "I'm sorry, I'm so sorry."

"Don't worry about it," I told him. "We need to go. Come on."

Ten minutes later, we were tumbling out of the car in front of Illinois Masonic. I left the car, not worrying about whether I got ticketed or towed. This was a very different approach to the building than what I'd used just a few hours before.

Joseph had thrown up on the way, but had been careful to do it in the bag I'd given him. He tried to be discreet, but it sparked a rash of gagging. Ross was the sickest. Brian and I supported him as we walked into the E.R. Of course, they couldn't take everyone at once. So Ross got to go first.

The triage nurse came out and spoke to me. I explained about the cookies, she nodded several times. "I'll take those for safe keeping," she said of the cookies I'd brought. "And I'll be back in just a minute or two."

I hoped when she said 'safe keeping' she meant under lock and key. It wouldn't do to have any of their staff mistake the cookies for actual treats.

The nurse came back five minutes later with another taller nurse. The taller one handed out basins to puke in, while the triage nurse poured out doses of liquid charcoal into Dixie cups. When she got to me, I told her, "I didn't have any cookies."

"All right. Do you know your friend's medical history?"

"Ross? Kind of."

"I do," Brian said, his mouth black with charcoal. "Is he okay?"

"He's conscious but a little groggy. We're giving him fluids. If you feel well enough to come back it might be helpful."

Franklin had a somewhat stricken look on his face but just said, "Go."

I looked at Joseph who was struggling to drink his charcoal. He said, "I think the cure might be worse than the disease."

"I'm sorry."

"What are you sorry about?"

"I keep putting your life in danger," I said.

"No, you don't. This was something out of your control."

"If you'd never met me, you'd be safe."

"You don't know that." He rubbed my knee. "Nick, life is dangerous. If you hide from danger, you hide from life."

Then he swallowed the rest of the charcoal. It might have been easier to take him seriously if his lips weren't black.

"Oh God, it's gritty." He made a face and said, "Go move the car. You don't want it to get towed."

I left, but instead I went into the emergency room and found Ross and Brian. Ross was pale and still. A doctor was shining a flashlight into his eyes.

"Nick, this is Dr. Schmidt," Brian said.

The young doctor glanced over his shoulder at me. "Do you know what kind of poison was in the cookies?"

"I was going to ask you the same thing," I said.

"My guess would be some kind of over-the-counter pesticide or rat killer. In general, it takes a lot to kill an adult human. Whatever it was, the dose was pretty low."

"So whoever did this just wanted to make us sick?"

"Not necessarily. They don't put instructions on the box for this kind of thing. Whoever did this might have thought they'd kill the whole bunch of you."

"So we don't know much at all."

"Only that your friends will be okay."

"Thanks."

With that, I ran outside to move my car. Fortunately, I didn't have a ticket, so I just pulled the Versailles into the parking garage across the way, figuring it would be worth the five or six dollars I'd have to pay when it was time for us all to go home.

I sat in the parked car for a minute or two. The terror of what had just happened began to seep in. I fought it, didn't have time for it. I forced it away, got out of the car, and went back into the hospital.

By the time I got back to the E.R., a gray Crown Vic sat in the illegal spot I'd just vacated. Inside, I looked around for whoever went with the unmarked car. It took a moment, but I eventually I saw Lieutenant Hamish Gardner standing at the information desk badgering a volunteer.

In the seventies, I knew Gardner as a sergeant on patrol.

He was in his late forties; a typical Irish cop who drank too much, swore too much, and pushed too many people around. He'd lost a lot of weight since the last time I saw him; a lot. His body looked like a half-empty paper bag.

"Hamish," I greeted him.

He stared at me for a long moment.

"Nowak. I heard you were dead."

"I'm a private investigator."

"Same difference."

"Are you here for the poisoning?" I asked, ignoring the snide remarks.

"Is that you? You look healthy enough."

"Someone left Christmas cookies outside my apartment door. My friends ate them. The nurse has the leftovers in a safe place."

"And you just let your friends eat them?"

"I wasn't there."

"All right, do you have any idea who left the cookies?"

"Yes. But I think I was the target."

"No shit. Tell me."

"Rita Lindquist. She's a private investigator."

"Never heard of her."

I shrugged. "She works the financial district mostly." I didn't know if that was entirely true. I only knew of the one client. My client. "She does work for Peterson-Palmer. She brings cookies in for everyone there."

"Are they usually poisoned?"

"No but—"

"That's all you've got? Fuck."

"I've been looking into her boyfriend. He's a financial planner. He's trying pull off some kind of Ponzi scheme."

"So you think she tried to poison you to fuck up your investigation?"

"Yes."

"That's it? She doesn't like you and she bakes cookies."

"Just go talk to her."

"No. I'm going to need more than that."

"You don't need probable cause to talk to someone."

"No. But I need it to cover my ass. I need to be able to explain myself if that someone complains to the chief of police, or an alderman, or God-forbid the fucking mayor."

She did seem like the sort who might resort to exactly that. If she couldn't get something on Gardner to blackmail him with, that is.

"Well, at least, run her name, check her license. You know, the basic stuff you guys do to me."

"Sure. What the fuck," he said. "What did you say her name was?"

"Rita. Rita Lindquist."

Chapter Ten

PEOPLE WHO PLAY with poison don't get violent. Or at least that's what I kept telling myself. I knew Vincent had already left for the holiday, but I still called and told his answering machine what had happened and asked that he call me when he got the message.

Ross spent the night in the hospital and the rest of us stayed at my place. Brian and Franklin on the pullout, Terry on the floor in a pile of blankets and pillows, and Joseph and I in the bedroom.

We could have all stayed at Brian's, but his sofa was famously uncomfortable—something I knew all too well having slept on it for more than a month. He really needed to buy something a human being could sleep on.

The next morning, none of us stirred until just after noon. We'd been at the hospital until after midnight. They finally took Franklin into the emergency room. That left Brian flitting between Ross and Franklin. Terry and Joseph were sick enough to be there, but didn't need much care from a doctor. Gardner took the remaining cookies and left. I was left sitting there in a rage.

I was showered and dressed before Joseph woke up asking, "Where are you going?"

"How do you feel?"

"Like someone marched an army through my gut. Where are you going?" he repeated.

"I have to do something about this."

"Isn't that what the police are for?"

"There's a difference between what they're for and what they'll do."

"Do you know who poisoned us?"

"I think so. I told Detective Gardner, but he's not going to do shit."

"So you have to." The look on his face told me he wanted to stop me. Didn't want me leaving. But knew I'd go anyway so all he said was, "Be safe, Nick."

"Try to call the hospital later and check on Ross."

"I will. I'll go down in a little bit."

"Only if you feel up to it," I said.

He chuckled.

"What?"

"Nothing. I'll take care of Ross. You go find the person who tried to hurt us."

Me, I thought, *she was trying to hurt me.* And she had. By hurting my friends.

When I got outside, I walked down the block to Melrose where I'd left the Versailles. It was very cold, and very windy. My trench coat blew in the wind like a sail and I was glad I'd worn a thermal T-shirt underneath a flannel button-down.

I was about to open the driver's door, when I realized I'd be better off leaving the car where it was. Rita probably knew what kind of car I drove. And the fact that the color of the Lincoln was on the distinctive side didn't help matters.

I pulled my coat tight around my neck and walked over to Broadway and then up to Addison where there was an Avis car rental. They only had one car for rent, but it wasn't bad. It was a greyish 1985 Oldsmobile Omega. It wasn't too big or too small. And it definitely wasn't memorable.

I had what I thought was Rita's address on Pine Grove, 3613 N. Pine Grove 2F, which as it turned out was only a block or two away from the rental place. So, I pulled around the block and began scouring the street for a parking spot. I found one about half a block away from Rita's building on the same side of the street. It wasn't ideal, but I knew there would be opportunities to move closer later on.

I was facing away from Rita's building, so I adjusted the review mirror and the side mirrors in order to see the front of Rita's building. It was a red brick courtyard building that had probably gone condo. The reason I thought it was a condo was that they'd put an ugly wrought iron fence across the front with brass colored call boxes next to the two gates. It was enough for a real-estate agent to call it a security building without actually providing anything resembling security. Just the kind of thing buyers paid extra for.

It was quarter to one and I settled in for a long boring day. Trying to watch someone was a pretty awful thing in the best weather. On a frigid winter day it was horrible. Not only was it freezing, but I was incredibly conspicuous. A man sitting in a car for hours was strange enough. Doing it in twenty-degree weather was menacing. The trick was to look busy, to look like I'd just parked and needed to do one or two little things in the car before going inside.

I dug my little notebook out of a pocket in my coat, found a pen in another and made a list of things I needed to take care of. I needed to reach Vincent Renaldi and catch him up on things. There was also a very important question I had to answer for myself: Had she been trying to kill me and failed or had she just wanted to frighten me off? Terry may have had the most cookies, though all he would say was 'a lot.' Franklin admitted to eight, so Terry probably had more than eight. Neither of them had been sick enough to spend the night in the hospital.

It was hard to imagine one person eating more than a dozen cookies in one sitting. And it seemed like you'd need the whole batch to kill you. So, was she simply inept? Or had the whole point been to taunt and terrorize? Or possibly distract?

I should talk to Sugar, too, I realized. I needed to tell her what I knew and then postpone the rest of her investigation until after I wrapped things up with Rita Lindquist. Whether Rita was trying to scare me or just simply bad at murder didn't matter. I had to keep my attention on her until she wasn't a threat anymore.

I glanced at the mirrors. Nothing going on. I didn't exactly know what Rita looked like, which could be a problem. People said she had frizzy hair, big boobs and a bossy attitude. All of which might be hard to spot through a rearview mirror half a block away. I was counting on her coming out of the building with Bill Appleton. I was fairly certain I'd recognize him from the wedding picture his wife had on her TV.

Of course, it hadn't occurred to me that their mode of transportation would be the big tip-off. I'd been there a little more than an hour—starting the engine every ten or fifteen minutes to clear the fog off the windows—when I saw a black limo pull up in front of the condo. I started the car and waited.

After a few minutes, a young couple scurried out of the building and into the limo. I barely got a look at them. It might have been Bill Appleton. The woman, though, I couldn't see much beyond a gigantic fur coat and a knit hat with a few gigantic sequins sewn onto it. The driver came around and got back into the car. As soon as it passed me, I pulled out onto Pine Grove and fell in behind it.

We stayed on Pine Grove to Cornelia, then turned toward the lake. At the inner drive, we turned right. We went down to Belmont, passing right by my apartment. Then, just below Belmont we fed onto Lake Shore Drive.

I stayed close to the limousine, not at all worried they'd figure out I was following them. They'd looked too comfortable, too confident. Lincoln Park was on one side of us and rows of residential skyscrapers were on the other. I tried not to wonder where we were going. When you followed someone like this, it didn't pay to think about the destination. The only thing that mattered was keeping up with them and being ready to move when they moved. We passed Diversey Harbor, Fullerton, the Lincoln Park Zoo, North Avenue Beach. Then we were getting into the right lane, Oak Street Beach on the left, Michigan Avenue in front of us.

Christmas shopping? I wondered. Is that what they were doing? Together? A young couple like that, you'd think the main people they were buying for would be each other. Almost as soon as we were on Michigan we stopped to wait for the left signal so we could turn onto Delaware Place, a one-way street running between the Hancock and the Westin. The signal was only green for a micro-second and I had to practically run the light to keep up with them. We went down Delaware Place, passing the residential entrance to the Hancock, then turned right on Dewitt and right again on Chestnut. The limousine pulled to the curb, and Bill Appleton and Rita Lindquist jumped out of the vehicle and ran into the Hancock. That left me having to find a place to park and figure out where they might have gone.

I was forced to drive around the block. I knew the Hancock, so it wasn't hard to figure out where they were going. The first forty-two or forty-three floors were businesses. You reached them by going in through the front entrance. The next fifty floors were condos. The residential entrance was on the north side of the building. The south side of the building, where they went in, allowed people to get to the observation deck, the restaurant and the bar. I doubted they were going to the observation deck, they were Chicagoans; you really didn't do that unless you had out of town guests. So they were there for a drink or a meal.

I had to park the car and get in there. The most expedient thing to do was park at the Hancock, so that's what I did, even though before I entered the six-story spiral a sign told me I'd be paying six dollars an hour. And I'd thought eight dollars for the day was expensive. I didn't expect to be in there long, though, so I took the ticket and drove the rental up the spiral. On the sixth floor I found a space, crossed my fingers that I'd be able to find the bland little car again, and went to find an elevator. That had me wandering around for about ten minutes until I finally found one—they really needed more signs—and I took it down to the first floor.

When I got to the main lobby, I did find a sign that led me to the side lobby where you caught the elevator to the observation deck and the cleverly named 95th, the restaurant on the 95th floor. On the floor above the restaurant was a bar called Images. Well, that was the official name. It was just as often called Top of the 'Cock.

When I got into the elevator with a group of obvious tourists, there were three buttons to choose from: 94, 95 and 96. On a hunch, I started with 96, Images. It was about three, which made it more likely Bill and Rita had come for a cocktail rather than a meal.

The ride up was very fast, making some of the out-of-towners ooh and ah. Most of them got out at the deck, and by the time we got to Images I was alone in the car. I stepped out into a foyer area with a coat check to my left and a host stand in front of me.

"Welcome to Images," a prissy young man in a tuxedo said when I walked that way. "Would you like to check your coat, sir?"

"I'm meeting some people. If they're here, sure. But if they're not, I won't stay."

He got a sour look on his face. He didn't like it, but I could see he didn't think it was worth fighting over. "Very well. Let me know if there's anything I can do for you."

I pushed by him into the bar. I zipped through, the long bar on one side, marble café tables and banquettes on the other, and beyond that the view. Scanning the room, I didn't see Bill or Rita anywhere. I kept going. Turning around the corner, I suddenly found myself staring at the restaurant below. The bar only took up part of the floor; the other part opened onto the restaurant, giving it an open airy feeling that was a bit discomforting with the stunning view of the city as a backdrop. An open stairway zigzagged its way down to the dining room.

Half of the tables still had diners. Shoppers having an elegant late lunch, I suppose. Suddenly, I recognized someone I knew in the center of the room. Gloria Silver sat behind a martini nibbling an hors d'oeuvre. Next to her were a couple of small wrapped gifts waiting to be given. She was having lunch with a young couple and it took me a moment to recognize that they were Bill and Rita.

And that didn't make any sense.

There was no reason in the world for these three to be together. And yet they were. The building seemed to sway as I stood there, and in fact it probably was swaying. It was windy outside and the building was meant to move an inch this way, an inch that. I stepped away from the railing a couple of feet so it would be harder to see me if they looked up.

They were having a lovely time, smiling at one another and laughing every now and then. It was my first chance to get a really good look at Rita Lindquist. She looked familiar. I'd definitely seen her before. She was trying to look elegant; she'd pulled back her obviously unruly hair and was wearing a silky blouse with a deep V that made the most of her assets.

Then I placed her. She'd been wearing a wig, and a coat that was too big and made her look dumpy. She'd been carrying too many shopping bags. She was the suburban woman looking at boy's shoes in Field's the day I followed Sugar around. Rita Lindquist was Gloria's spy.

I turned and left the bar. When I got back to the ground, I knew what I had to do to start making sense out of this. Leaving the rental where it was, I went out to Michigan Avenue, walked four very chilly blocks north to Cedar, and rang Sugar Pilson's bell.

Gretchen answered. I could tell that she wanted to turn me away, probably for good, but she let me in as far as the foyer.

"Wait here," she said, and then climbed the stairs to the second floor.

Two minutes later, Sugar stood at the top of the stairs in just a bra and panties. "Nick, darling, come up. I'm getting ready for this horrid party tonight."

I climbed the stairs to the second floor and by the time I got to the top she was all the way down the hallway already. She waved at me to follow and then went into what I presumed was her bedroom.

When I entered the room, I saw that her bedroom had once been two rooms at the front of the house. Someone, probably Sugar, had removed a wall between the rooms and now one of them was half sitting room, half dressing room. Gretchen fussed with three dresses spread over a sofa in the sitting room half. There were also a hair stylist named Philip, with floppy hair and a penchant for buying his clothes in the boys department; and a makeup artist named Garth, a giant Kewpie doll of a man standing next to Sugar at the make-up table.

"I'm sorry," Sugar said. "I'm running terribly late."

"What time is the party?" I asked.

"It starts at seven. There's a red carpet with photos so I've got to be on time."

"It's not even four o'clock."

"Oh God, don't say things like that," Sugar squealed.

I almost asked her if it always took her three hours to get dressed, but I knew it didn't. The difference was the red carpet.

"If you're going to upset her you'll have to leave," Garth said. "You have no idea how difficult it is to make someone up who's frowning."

"You're right. I have no idea. Sugar, we need to talk. Confidentially."

"Now?"

"Ten minutes. Maybe fifteen."

"You can't just tell me? We could change the names to protect the innocent."

"Someone dropped off poison cookies at my apartment last night."

"Are you serious? Are you all right?"

"I didn't have any but everyone else did. Ross is still in the hospital."

"Oh my Lord, that's awful! Gretchen, we need to send Ross flowers." Turning back to me, she said, "But that can't have anything to do with the matter I asked you to look into."

"I didn't think so, but I just saw something that changed my mind."

Sugar sat back and thought for a moment. "All right. Gretchen take the boys downstairs and give them a cocktail."

"Cocktails? Sugar, really? You know what happened—"

"Cookies and milk, then. Nick and I need a few minutes alone."

Everyone left the room. Sugar got up and walked over to the sofa. She made a space between her dresses and sat down. Then she pointed at a comfortable looking chair and said, "Darling, sit down. If you're going to ruin my life you should be comfortable."

I sat down, and I was much more comfortable.

"I'm going to backtrack a little, but I'll get to what I just saw in a minute. Did you know Michael France is actually Michael Francelli?"

"Yes, of course I knew that."

"Michael Francelli was involved in an art fraud while he was still a student at the Art Institute."

"Oh." She clearly didn't know that. "Well, that explains a few things. He talked about a youthful indiscretion once. Silly me, I thought he was talking about sex."

"He and Gloria own his house jointly."

"Well, that he never mentioned."

"And it's paid for. So it's not like she co-signed for a mortgage."

"Well that doesn't make me happy, but I don't—"

"So, you know the other case I'm working on? The one with the financial planner who's kind of fishy?"

"Yes, of course. That was so much fun—"

"I'm pretty sure he's running some kind of Ponzi scheme with mutual funds."

"Really?"

"I just saw him. At the 95th with his girlfriend and Gloria Silver having a snack and exchanging Christmas gifts."

Sugar was stunned. Then she asked, "What do you think that means?"

"His girlfriend is Rita Lindquist, the investigator. I recognized her from the day we were at Field's. She was following us around, but she looked like any other shopper so I didn't think anything about it. That means she's working for Gloria."

"You said she took your old job."

"Yes, she did. She showed up one day and blackmailed her way into it."

"Gloria hates you, doesn't she?"

"She hates us both. She's using Rita to mess with you."

"Yes, I see that. But, she can't use the column against you. You don't care about those things—unless I'm a terrible judge of character."

"No, I don't care. Gloria must have hired Rita Lindquist some time after Earl's funeral."

She'd seen me there with Ross and taken a strong dislike to us both. She may have learned early on that fate was punishing Ross, which left me. Of course, fate had hardly been kind to me, but she might not understand that.

How long had Rita been following me around? Had she been there in the background when I was trying to solve Roland Meek's murder? Had she been at Bert's funeral? I couldn't tell you. I could barely remember any of that day, and what I could remember was full of gaps. What about when I worked at Irving's "L" Lounge? Had she come in dressed like some cheap, slutty drunk just to watch me pour beer? Did she track me as I worked the Jimmy English case? Was she always there just at the edge of my peripheral vision?

It was a creepy thing to think about.

I said, "I'm not really seeing how it all connects with the Ponzi scheme, though."

"What do you know about the financial planner?"

"He's not qualified. Didn't finish college. Lied about everything on his application. Supposedly Rita fell in love with him while she was doing the background check. They moved in together last year."

"And who can blame her. A man with credentials like that," Sugar said, tongue planted firmly in cheek.

"And then, I guess, she involved Gloria in the Ponzi scheme."

"Clearly. Gloria has wads of cash now."

"I don't know. It all just seems too—"

"Coincidental?"

"Yes."

"But Nick, you're forgetting something. Love is always a coincidence. Once you accept that, the rest makes perfect sense."

Chapter Eleven

I LEFT SUGAR'S, walked back to the Hancock and picked up the rental—finding it again made me feel like I'd won the Lotto. I drove back to the rental office in Boystown and turned the car in. The clerk gave me a funky look. I'd had the car for less than six hours and driven eleven miles. She had to be thinking I could have taken a cab for far less. I paid for a gallon of gas after she rounded up.

Afterward, I walked over to my office. The sun had set and the wind was beginning to die down. When it got dark that early I always had a strange sense of the day ending before it was meant to. Walking into my office, I found the air cold and stale. I hadn't been there in a while, so I turned on my space heater and flipped the switch on my answering machine so I could listen to my messages. Three hang-ups and a man named O'Hara who wanted me to call back with my rates.

The hang-ups gave me the creeps. Were they from yesterday? Was it Rita checking to see if I was in my office? Was she trying to figure out whether to leave the cookies here?

What about all the other hang-ups over the last year? Were they Rita, too? It was a disturbing thought.

I lit a cigarette and thought about how I wanted all this to turn out. Actually, that part was pretty easy. What I wanted, what I really wanted, was for Rita Lindquist and her boyfriend to go to prison. It would be nice if Gloria went with them and it would be nice if all that happened without Vincent Renaldi losing his job.

Of course, Rita wasn't just going to let that happen. She would try to stop me. In fact, the cookies may have been meant as a warning. If I kept trying to put her in prison she'd probably keep trying to hurt me.

I had to think about where I was vulnerable. What could she do to me that might actually make me stop? Her specialty was blackmail. There were very few things in my life that would make me succumb; in fact, probably none. It wasn't that I was an angel, it was that I simply didn't care anymore what people knew about me. Joseph knew my darkest secrets and still loved me. And my job was not dependent on anyone's good opinion. In fact, in my profession a little bit of bad was a good thing.

To stop me Rita would have to kill me and—despite her foray into baked goods—I wasn't sure she could kill. Damage, maim, harass, threaten, blackmail, those were her tools of the trade. Murder? I wasn't so sure.

I wondered exactly who I'd be turning Rita and Bill over to. The FBI? The FDIC? The Chicago Board of Trade? I should probably leave that part up to Vincent. Yeah, that's what I should do. Vincent needed to be the hero so that if Rita's blackmail came out—and it probably would—he'd stand a chance of keeping his job.

As far as I could tell though, not much was going to happen until Wednesday. I had four days to get my ducks in a row. Well, in-between taking Mrs. Harker to holiday meals and the doctor. I wondered if I should try to find out more about Appleton's clients. What did they have in common? Were they all older like Edward Johnstone's father? And how did he find them? That would be a good thing to know.

Then I had an interesting thought. If the blackmail was going to come out anyway, maybe I could convince Vincent to turn Rita in to the police for blackmailing him. The CPD wouldn't like it much because there wasn't any money involved. But when you blackmail someone for a job it's still a felony. I wondered if he'd go for it. I made a mental note to call him about that.

First though, I picked up the phone and called home.

"Hey," I said when Joseph picked up.

"Hey yourself."

"How are you feeling?"

"I'm okay."

"Did you get to see Ross?"

"Yeah, he'll be home tomorrow. There were some extra tests the doctor wanted to do since they have him anyway. But he's feeling a lot better."

"And the rest of the sick ward?"

"They went home. Brian's feeling good enough to go to Lu's party tonight."

"Did you want to go?"

"No. I'm not up to drinking. You can go if you want."

"I think I'll pass. I'm coming home now. You want me to pick something up?"

"Soup?"

"Soup it is."

After saying good-bye, I walked over to the Melrose and ordered two chicken soups with extra crackers to go. Then I wondered if there were bagels for breakfast. Crap, maybe I should have swung by Treasure Island first. It was too late, though. I wasn't going to wander around Boystown in the dark with a bag full of chicken soup.

Then I had a funky thought that had nothing to do with food. What if Gloria was the connection? What if she'd introduced Bill to Rita? What if she sent him into Peterson-Palmer knowing what he'd do there? She had to be a part of the Ponzi scam, an important part, since she was getting a big cut.

Twenty minutes later, Joseph and I sat down at the little table in front of my big window looking out at the lights of Chicago's North Side. He'd cleaned the apartment and you'd never know that five men had slept there the night before, no less that most of them had puked at least once. The soup was still hot and I crumbled three packages of crackers into mine.

The heat was on a bit too high, so I cranked open one of the windows.

"Don't leave it like that," Joseph warned. "I don't want it to freeze open."

I wanted to say that wouldn't happen, but I wasn't sure it wouldn't. I'd never left one open all night when it was this cold.

"Explain this to me again," Joseph said. "The woman who you think poisoned us took your old job, but she also works for Gloria Silver."

I didn't always tell Joseph what I was working on, but since he'd eaten one of the poisoned cookies he'd become part of the case and I thought it unfair to keep things from him.

"I'm guessing that Gloria hired Rita Lindquist sometime after Earl's funeral. And she's been keeping an eye on me."

"Why does Gloria Silver hate you so much?"

"I know that her husband didn't die of liver disease like it says in his obituary. I know that he died of AIDS."

"Why does that make a difference? He's still dead."

"She would be terribly humiliated it if ever came out."

Joseph sipped his soup and ruminated. I think he had trouble understanding the anger, hatred and resentment Gloria must feel to do these things. But then, he must have run across it in the confessional. It wasn't *that* uncommon.

"Do you think Gloria ordered this Rita person to poison us?"

"Me. She was aiming for me."

Joseph cocked his head. "You don't strike me as the Christmas cookie-eating sort, Nick."

"Rita Lindquist has never met me."

"She's been following you a long time, though. Earl died two and a half years ago. She has to have some sense of who you are."

We slurped our soup in the most disgusting way.

"How do you know when Earl died?"

"Well, it was in the newspaper and, you know, Ross talks about him."

"Does he?"

"Yes, Nick, he talks about him all the time. Do you think Earl gave Gloria AIDS? He gave it to Ross."

I stopped eating and lit a cigarette. I thought about it. Finally, I said, "I have no reason to think that. She seems healthy enough. But honestly I don't know."

"How does she have the money for a private eye? Do they pay that much for her column?"

"I don't think they do. I'm pretty sure she's in on the Ponzi scheme."

Joseph pushed his soup away. Finished. He looked at me for a moment then he took my cigarette away from me and rubbed it out in the ashtray.

"You know what? We're alone. We could fuck in the living room."

"You're right. I guess we could."

He leaned across the table and kissed me. He was salty from the crackers. Moving closer to me he nearly sat in my lap, but that would have collapsed the wooden folding chair I sat on. I pulled us down to the floor and we kept kissing.

I loved kissing him. And part of me wanted to do only that. If I could just kiss him forever then there wouldn't be any challenging decisions. Just kissing.

Slipping my hands under his sweater, I found his nipples and pinched them. He moaned, but that didn't stop him from unbuttoning my flannel shirt. I pinched, he moaned, and he slipped my shirt over my shoulders and then pulled my thermal T-shirt over my head.

The carpet was scratchy and unpleasant, so I spread the T-shirt out so we could lie on it. Then I pulled off Joseph's sweater. We kissed some more and pressed our bare chests together. After a bit, we shimmied out of our jeans.

I took both our cocks into one hand and jerked them, rubbing them together. He kissed me harder. I rolled on top of him and ground my dick into his. Taking our pricks into my hand again, I made a sort of tunnel with my palm and fingers that we could both fuck. I thrust into it.

He wrapped his legs around me and whispered into my ear, "Fuck me."

I wanted to. I really wanted to. But I knew from reading Brian's brochures three and four and five times, that it was probably the most dangerous thing we could do. Then I got an idea. I hopped up and went to the tiny kitchen/closet and reached into the cabinet to get out a bottle of vegetable oil. I brought it over to Joseph and got back onto the floor with him.

"Nick?"

I turned him on his side, nearly face down, giving myself a lovely view of his ass and thighs. "Hold your thighs together." I opened the vegetable oil and carefully poured it onto his ass and legs. Then I began rubbing it around.

"You're basting my thighs. Are you going to put me in the oven?"

"I read about this in one of Brian's brochures. It's called frottage."

"Nick, this is silly. Just get a condom and fuck me."

"Shush."

"Or get a condom and let me fuck you," he teased. He knew that wasn't my thing.

Ignoring him, I slid my dick between his slick thighs. It wasn't unpleasant and it was certainly guilt free. Reaching around I grabbed his dick in my oily hand. I slid a thumb into his ass and he stopped talking.

While he kept his thighs clenched I moved back and forth. His breathing got faster. He reached back and ran his hand across my chest. I let go of him and placed a hand on his left thigh and pushed down so that it was even tighter around my dick. Then I pumped him hard and fast.

Taking his hand away from my chest he began jerking himself off. I tried to wait for him, but it was too sweet. I came, my cum jetting between his thighs, landing on his fist as it bobbed up and down on his cock. He gasped when he saw it happen and just a few seconds later he was coming himself.

Later, we lay on our discarded clothes staring at the ceiling. "You missed Friday night," I pointed out. "Should we have two next week?"

"Do you need two?"

"No."

"Then I'm fine."

"We could have zero?" I suggested.

"My therapist says I'm in my gay adolescence."

That wasn't an answer to my question, nor did I know

what to make of it, so I joked, "Are you telling me I'm a pervert?"

"No, I'm trying to understand myself. I'm trying to help you understand me." I thought he was finished but then he added, "You use humor to deflect."

"If you psychoanalyze me, I'm going to punch you."

"Violence? Really?"

"Look, we're going to have a problem if the only response I can give you is, 'Oh, goodie.'"

"Point taken."

We were silent for a moment, then he rolled over and whispered, "I don't think you're a pervert, Nick. I *know* you are." And then he bit my ear.

———

SUNDAY MORNING the weather was almost balmy, tipping over forty degrees. Ross called at eight to say he could come home, so Joseph and I were out of the apartment by eight-thirty. We found the Versailles on Melrose and drove to Illinois Masonic.

On the way, Joseph said, "We should have a plan."

"A plan for what?"

"Christmas dinner. It's only two days away, you know."

"Oh yeah, we need to go shopping, don't we?"

"Don't worry about that. I'll take care of it. We need a plan for Mrs. Harker, though."

"Oh. I've been trying not to think about that." Actually, I'd been a little busy and trying *not* to think about it. Luckily, those two things worked hand in hand.

"Are you going to tell her about me? You know, before you go pick her up."

"She won't come if I do."

"It's really not fair just to spring it on her."

"It's not fair leaving her alone either." I might have been a little snappish when I said that. "There isn't a fair way to do this. If there was we'd do it that way."

"You're worried about her, aren't you?"

"I think she might be very ill."

We parked in the garage across from the ER and entered the hospital. We went to the elevator and Joseph pressed three. We wound down one long hallway and then another. I had a moment's fear we were going to find Ross shoved into some tiny little backroom where the nurses had been handling him with tongs or some other ridiculous precaution to match the horror stories we'd heard.

But it wasn't like that. When we got to him, Ross was in a large room that had four beds. The room was bright and clean. Nurses flitted around without any special hazard gear other than big smiles. Ross sat on the edge of his bed, wearing his own pajamas. His winter coat sat next to him. On the small table next to his bed was a very large poinsettia.

"Hey, buddy, how are you?"

"They want to start radiation on my neck."

"Okay." I'd gotten so used to the lesions on his neck. I barely saw them.

"It's twice a week."

"Okay. We'll get you here," Joseph said.

"Yeah, don't worry about it."

Ross looked away. I had the feeling he was thinking about how inconvenient he was to have around. I didn't know how to tell him it didn't matter. That not having him around would be so much worse. Joseph sat on the bed next to him and rested a hand on his.

Dr. Macht walked in. "Looks like someone's going home."

"It's Sunday, what are you doing here?" I asked.

"Don't worry. I'm only working half a day. How are the rest of you doing? I heard you had a bad batch of cookies."

"We did," I said.

"Nick was smart enough not to eat any of them," Ross said.

"I don't know if I was that smart. There were hardly any left when I got there."

"Well, it's put me off holiday baking, that's for sure. Or at least eating anything I find outside my front door," Dr. Macht said. "Do they know who did it?"

"Not yet," I said, the simplest answer.

"Well, the nurse will be in with your discharge papers in just a minute. And I'll see you on Friday." Nodding at Ross. And to me he said, "And you on Thursday."

"No," I said. "I think it's the other way around. You're seeing me on Friday."

Ross nodded.

Dr. Macht smiled and said, "This is why someone else keeps my appointment book."

After he left, Ross gave me a quizzical look. "Friday?"

"Mrs. Harker."

He nodded.

Something nagged at me. I hadn't heard back from Vincent Renaldi. I probably shouldn't worry. He was out of town. And maybe he didn't have the kind of answering machine you could check from anywhere. Or maybe he'd gotten my message and just hadn't bothered to call me. Or maybe something was wrong. On the nightstand between the two beds on this side of the room, there a beige desk phone.

"Does that phone work?"

"Local only. Dial 9."

I nodded and picked up the phone. Ross' roommate was a black kid, emaciated and angry-looking. I was tempted to smile at him, but wasn't sure he'd appreciate it. I dialed my office.

A few months before I'd bought a new Panasonic answering machine. It came with a plastic remote that made a beeping noise into the phone allowing you to hear your messages. I took the remote out of a pocket and beeped it into the phone when the machine picked up. I had no messages. I shoved it back into a pocket and dialed Vincent's home number. No answer. Not even a machine. That was odd. On Friday there had been a machine.

The nurse came in with Ross' discharge papers, which she had him sign. They brought a wheelchair. Ross got into the chair along with the large poinsettia and an orderly walked us out of the hospital.

"Where did the flowers come from?" I asked.

"Sugar."

Gretchen was efficient. I wondered if the card said, 'Get well soon' and 'Merry Christmas.' Walking close to Joseph I leaned in to say, "I'm just going to drop you off. There are some things I need to do."

"We'll be fine."

On the drive, Joseph caught Ross up on everything he'd missed being in the hospital, which really wasn't much.

"You should call Brian," I said. "I think he's free tonight and he'll want to see you."

Ross didn't answer, just looked out the window. He and Brian were still close, but I wondered if Ross didn't still harbor feelings for Brian. What-if feelings if nothing else.

I pulled the Versailles over to the curb and Joseph got out to help Ross. Once Ross was safely on the sidewalk, Joseph stuck his head back into the car.

"Be careful, Nick."

"I'm always careful."

"Yeah, be more careful."

I nodded and pulled away. He'd been telling me that a lot and it was starting to annoy me. Yes, it was true that I'd been shot at a couple of times in October, and I took a nasty beating in August, and I did get myself stabbed right before we'd started dating. I mean, I guess that was excessive for most people. But I was just doing my job and I actually had been careful. In fact, he should probably stop telling me to be careful. Bad things happened when I was careful.

Vincent lived on Belden below Fullerton. I should have probably parked and taken a cab or even a bus, it would have been easier. I rode down the Inner Drive, through Diversey Harbor and then cut over when I got to Fullerton. As soon as I turned onto Lincoln Park West, I began looking for some place to put the car. I found a place in front of a soccer field, then doubled back to Belden. On Vincent's street, I walked down the block until I got near his building. It was a stone and brick, three-story building that was two apartments wide and about ten apartments deep. I remembered that Vincent lived in one of the studios toward the back and that the kitchen was only big enough for a stove, the sink and a couple of cupboards. He had to keep his refrigerator in the main room.

I was barely twenty feet down Belden when I saw there was a commotion in front of his building. There were several squads and a coroner's van. I started saying "fuck" under each breath as I picked up my pace. Something had happened to Vincent.

When I was on the job I did a lot of securing of crime scenes. I imagined that was true for the uniform standing in front of Vincent's building. Maybe if I'd started the conversation in another way we could have bonded.

"Is Vincent Renaldi dead?" I asked. "He's dead, isn't he?"

"I can't release any information."

"It's Vincent Renaldi. What happened to him?"

"I don't know who's in there or what this is about. I'm just here to secure the crime scene, which you're a little too close to."

I stepped back. He was right. They wouldn't be rushing out every few minutes to keep him up to date. All he really knew was not to let anyone into the building. And if he knew more than that, he knew not to share it.

I lit a cigarette and paced in front of the building for a while. Then I went back over to the uniform and asked him, casually, "How long have you been out here?"

He looked at me, deciding whether it was an innocuous enough question that he could answer it. He looked at the big clunky watch on his wrist. "Since about almost noon."

A little more than an hour. I wondered if they were already in the apartment when I called? Had they unplugged the answering machine? The phone?

"Who's lead on this? Is it Gardner?"

That question wasn't innocuous enough. "Who are you?"

"Nick Nowak. Private investigator."

"You have information to share?"

"I might. Are you here because of Vincent Renaldi?"

"Why do you think it might be your friend?"

"He lives in this building and he hasn't been answering the phone. And somebody tried to poison me with cookies just a few days ago."

I saw a flicker in his eye. Vincent had been poisoned. I wasn't sure that made sense, though. Rita hadn't done such a good job of poisoning us—if the point had been to kill me she'd totally screwed up. Plus, Vincent left town on Thursday. She left us cookies on Friday. Of course, she *could* have left Vincent cookies on Thursday. So, was he dead? Or had an ambulance already been there to take him away.

Just then Gardner came out of the building. He scowled when he saw me, but he came over anyway.

"Is Vincent Renaldi dead?" I asked.

He ignored me and said, "I met Rita Lindquist."

"You went and talked to her?" I was a little surprised by that.

"No, she came and talked to me. First thing this morning."

"Really?"

"Yeah, she had a lot to say about her boyfriend, Appleton."

The coroners came out of the building pushing a stretcher. Vincent Renaldi went by in a body bag. He was dead. I started mumbling "shit" again. "Shit, shit, shit." This shouldn't have happened. I didn't see how I could have stopped it, but, still, it shouldn't have happened.

"Yeah, Rita said he got shit-faced last night and confessed," Gardner went on. "She makes cookies every year and this year he dribbled antifreeze on them. And then dropped them off at your door and Renaldi's door."

"Why'd he do that?"

"She says he's crap at his job and that you and this Renaldi guy were figuring that out."

"So he murdered Vincent so he wouldn't lose his job?"

"I've heard of dumber reasons to kill someone."

"She's lying."

"Yeah, well, we've got them both over at Town Hall. So far he's confessing to everything she said."

"Then he's lying, too."

"Now why the fuck would he do that?"

"I don't know. But I do know that Vincent was going out of town on Thursday so that means the cookies were dropped off before then, and more cookies were dropped off at my place on Friday. That's a lot of planning, a lot of thought. I'll bet it's not as neat as they're making out."

"Lemme guess, you want me to look a gift horse in the mouth."

"No, Gardner, I want you to do your job."

"You know, it's not my fucking job to tell you shit. Keep that in mind."

He walked away.

Chapter Twelve

AS I WALKED BACK to my car, I thought, *Now I know what's going on, except I don't know what's going on.* Rita and Bill were up to something and I didn't know what. All I knew for sure was that Detective Gardner was happy they'd tied the whole thing up for him. I had the feeling it would all come crumbling down, but I couldn't figure out how or when.

I sat in the car for a few minutes, started the engine, told myself I was letting it warm up. It didn't seem real that Vincent was dead. I didn't know how to think about that. And I didn't know what to do next. I just focused on breathing for a while. In and out. In and out. And then I gave myself the same command I'd given Gardner: *Do your job.* And it was my job to make Rita and Bill pay for what they'd done.

I drove to my office, parked and let myself in. The landlord didn't really heat the place on Sunday, so I kept my coat on. I sat down at the desk and opened the Peterson-Palmer file. My first thought was to make a chart and show the way money magically disappeared whenever Appleton bought the phony mutual funds. But then I got another idea.

Who were these people and where did they come from? Instead of a chart, I made a list of the fifteen clients Bill had power of attorney over. The first two names were Paul Johnstone and Naomi Bellingham. The complainants.

Paul Johnstone was dead, so I looked up Naomi Bellingham in the phone book. I found an N. Bellingham at the right address in Evanston and dialed the number. After four rings, a woman answered.

"Hello?"

"Yes, Mrs. Bellingham?"

"Mrs.? Oh my," the woman said, before giggling. "I'm not a Mrs., I never married." The last bit was said with some surprise, as though she'd just remembered this fact.

"Ah, Miss Bellingham."

"Yes, I'm Miss Bellingham. Who is this, please?"

"I'm with Peterson-Palmer. I'm calling to let you know that Bill Appleton is no longer with us."

"Oh no. That isn't my fault is it? Because I was wrong. Terribly wrong. I didn't realize it until that nice young woman came to see me. She brought cookies. Delicious cookies."

I was tempted to say, "You're lucky you survived them."

"It wasn't your fault Miss Bellingham."

"Oh, thank goodness."

"If you don't mind me asking, how did you come to be Bill Appleton's client?"

"How did I—?"

"Yes, how did the two of you meet?"

"You know it's been some time. I can't say that I recall. You know, I went to church this morning."

"That's very nice."

"That means it's Sunday. You're working on a Sunday."

"Well, we felt it was very important to reach out to our clients."

"Oh. Well, that's so nice."

"Do you remember the last time you went down to the Loop?"

"The Loop? Well, I'm sure it's been years. There's an express train, you know. I used to take that, but, well, there are just too many stairs."

"You have trouble with stairs?"

"Oh yes, my knees aren't good anymore."

"How old are you Miss Bellingham?"

"You should never ask a woman that sort of question."

"Oh, I'm sorry. Getting back to financial matters how long have you been receiving Social Security?"

"Oh, ages. Twelve, thirteen years, I guess."

That put her around seventy-seven or seventy-eight. As for Paul Johnstone, I didn't know his age but put him in the same age bracket. His son was over forty, after all. I said good-bye to Naomi Bellingham. She thanked me for calling, though I doubted she was sure what the call was about.

I called the next two people on the list and got similar results. The first didn't seem to remember who Bill Appleton was at all. Disturbing when you remember Appleton had their financial power of attorney. And the second remembered Bill and was sure they went to college together. In 1943.

Then I called a gentleman named Karl Ackermann. He had a soft German accent, but otherwise spoke English perfectly. He was also sharp as a tack. After I introduced myself as being from Peterson-Palmer, I asked if he remembered how he'd met Bill Appleton."

"I remember very well, thank you. I met Bill Appleton through My Old Friend."

"Which old friend is that?"

"No. My Old Friend. The charity. They bring my dinner two times a week, and if I need a ride to the doctor they have taxi vouchers. And, well, they do all sorts of things."

"Like introduce you to Bill Appleton."

"Yes, exactly like that."

My heart was racing a bit, this was important. This meant something.

"Mr. Ackermann, can you tell me why you gave Appleton a power of attorney over your account?"

"I'm not sure why you're asking me that. That is not how the special account works?"

This should not have been surprised me. When Appleton couldn't convince people to sign legitimately, he just lied to them.

"Mr. Ackermann, Appleton has a limited power of attorney over your account. Now, you may have signed it thinking it was something else. Or Appleton may have just forged your signature."

"That all sounds very serious."

"It is. You should call tomorrow and have your account changed. And then you might want to call into question the decisions Bill Appleton made for you," I suggested. Flipping quickly through the statements, it looked like Appleton had cost him roughly a hundred and forty thousand dollars.

"Thank you. I will do that."

After I hung up, I spent the next hour calling everyone else on the list. I didn't bother saying that I was from Peterson-Palmer nor did I mention Bill Appleton. All I did was ask them what services they got from My Old Friend and how happy they were with the charity. People loved My Old Friend.

Then, to cross my T's and dot my I's, I called Paul Johnstone's son, Naomi Bellingham, and the two people I'd spoken to before I spoke to Karl Ackermann. They'd all used My Old Friend. They called it a "Godsend."

It was almost two o'clock and I was starving to death. I called Joseph and asked him to have lunch with me at the Melrose. He'd already eaten, but said he'd come by for a coffee. Before I left, though, I placed one more call.

"Tell me everything you know about the charity My Old Friend," I asked Sugar when she came to the phone.

"Well, I don't know much about it. But I do know who does…Gloria."

"Gloria? Gloria Silver?"

"Yes, it's her favorite charity. I mean, she shouldn't have a favorite, should she? She should be supporting all charities equally, but she's on the board of My Old Friend. They do a gala in the spring. Everyone goes. Why? What does that have to do with anything?"

"Gloria was sending old people to Bill Appleton. Rich old people."

————

"IT SEEMS like an awful thing to do, stealing from old people," Joseph said.

It took me a moment to respond since my mouth was full of bacon cheeseburger. "It's an awful thing to steal from anyone. It's just easier to steal from old people."

"Are you telling, um, what's the detective's name who's handling this?"

"Gardner."

"Are you going to tell Gardner?"

"I'm not sure it's enough, yet."

"It seems pretty convincing to me."

"Gloria could say it's all a coincidence. She could say that Bill Appleton took advantage of her."

"Did he?"

"She seems to have a lot of money. But then maybe she can explain the money."

"So you're not going to tell Gardner?"

"I will. Just not yet. I've got some other paperwork to do. I should have everything together before I do anything. Actually, I might go directly to the state's attorney's office on Wednesday." As soon as I said that I remembered Mrs. Harker was having a test, but maybe I could fit in both.

"Why don't you want to go sooner?"

"I imagine they're only open half a day tomorrow and closed on Tuesday. It's just easier. Besides, Bill and Rita are both in jail. I doubt they're going anywhere."

"Why do you think she didn't kill us?" he asked, seemingly out of nowhere. "I mean, she killed your friend Vincent. So why am I sitting here?"

For a moment, the idea of him not sitting there, not being alive brought me to a complete stop. I'd barely let myself think about what had almost happened. But there it was, in the terrifying words, "Why am I sitting here?"

"I don't know. It might have been a mistake. Maybe Vincent ate more of the cookies. Or maybe Vincent's health wasn't good and Rita just nudged him along."

"Franklin and Terry both ate a lot of cookies. And I think you would have noticed if his health was as bad as Ross'."

Those were good points that I couldn't refute, so I said, "It was anti-freeze. Rita says Bill is the one who put it on the cookies."

"Do you think that's the truth?"

I shrugged. "I don't know. It'll take weeks to find out for sure what was in the cookies. It happened Friday night. The cookies may not even be at the lab yet. The weekend and the holiday are going to slow things down. Actually, two holidays. And it's not a fast process to begin with."

"So we won't know. Not for a long time."

"We may never know, Joseph. The tests will tell us if the poison was anti-freeze. It might even tell us that there was a lot more in Vincent's batch. But it won't tell us whether it was deliberate or a mistake."

"We were there when she left the cookies, Ross and I. Later on, Brian, Franklin and Terry came and they brought the cookies in. I keep wondering if she listened at the door, if she heard the TV or me and Ross talking."

"You shouldn't think about it too much."

"It's just, if she listened to us, if she knew that we were real, that we were human, how could she do what she did?"

"Joseph, there are bad people in the world."

"I know that. Or, I know it logically, but maybe I don't want to believe it."

"No one wants to believe it."

After lunch, I went back to my office and very carefully charted the movements of money in and out of the three phony mutual funds that Appleton was using. The combined losses of the fifteen accounts he controlled was nearly three million dollars. Presumably, a similar amount of money came out of the mutual funds and into the pockets of Rita, Bill and Gloria.

Once I had everything neatly written out I typed it up. Typing up a chart is a horrible experience in the best circumstances, and since my fingers were getting frostbitten my circumstances were not the best.

At a Christmas party earlier in the month, someone was telling me—oh, God, it was Franklin—Franklin was telling me that there were programs you could get for a computer that would make a chart for you lickety-split. Something called Lotus, I think. I wondered if there might be a time, maybe in about a decade or so, when I actually might want a computer for tasks like this.

When I was all finished, I made a little stack of my chart, the statements, a written narrative of everything I knew, or thought I knew, and put it into a large manila envelope. I was ready to go to the state's attorney on Wednesday, which meant I had Christmas Eve and Christmas Day completely off.

Joseph had said he was going shopping for Christmas dinner. We'd have something simple like sandwiches and soup for our Sunday dinner. I thought about leaving the car where it was and just walking home, but even with Rita and Bill in jail I'd be happier if it was nearby.

But first, before I went home, I drove down to the video store on Addison and rented *Miracle on 34th Street*. I couldn't believe my luck. I hadn't expected there to be a single Christmas movie left, but then maybe people didn't care about black-and-white movies anymore. I did, though, and I was excited.

The movie was built on the idea that Santa Claus was real. And that was exactly what Joseph and I needed right now.

Chapter Thirteen

WHEN I LEFT my apartment the next morning, I picked up the *Daily Herald* off the mat and tucked it under my arm. I could read it while I was waiting for Mrs. Harker to have her test. Pulling up to her place in Edison Park, I found her on the curb again. It was lightly snowing, and the temperature was hovering around twenty degrees.

"It's too cold. Wait in the lobby until I get here. Then come out," I scolded her as she got into the car.

"Cold is good for circulation."

"No. Cold is bad for circulation. It constricts the blood vessels." I'd read that in the *Daily Herald*. Every year they published an article about why so many people dropped dead shoveling the first snowfall. It was the cold much more than the exertion that killed you.

She scowled at me. Then I realized she might not know the word constricts. "Tightens."

"Oh no, is not true. Cold brings energy. Hot brings sleep."

I decided not to argue with her. Instead I turned up the heat in the car. Maybe she'd take the hint and drift off.

A few blocks later she asked, "What does mean? Boy say you poison him?"

"I didn't poison him. A very bad woman left poisoned cookies on our doorstep. Terry ate some. So did my other friends."

"Is not smart to eat poison cookies."

"No, it's not. She left some for my boss. He died."

She frowned a moment and then seemed to relax into her seat, "You will find her."

"Yes, I will."

By the time we parked, walked across the street into Illinois Masonic, and found what they were calling Nuclear Medicine—not a reassuring name by the way—we were ten minutes late. The department was in a dark corner of the basement, as though pushed to one side for everyone's safety. A perky little girl in pink scrubs signed us in.

"We don't usually schedule anyone on the day before a holiday. We're really only open for emergencies." I glared at her until she said, "Oh, sorry. The good news is you won't have to wait long. Just fill out this form and I'll bring you in, and we'll put in the IV."

Mrs. Harker gave me a worried look.

"You're going to do everything you're asked. Now fill out the form." I almost asked her wouldn't she rather have an IV than an enema but figured the less said the better.

She tightened her jaw as though she were about to defy me so I opened the newspaper and started to read. Terrorists had bombed a train in Italy, two hundred people were injured and more than two dozen died. Groups on both the left and the right claimed responsibility for the bombing. Reagan continued to steal from the poor and give to the rich. An unknown man shot four teenagers on a New York subway claiming they tried to mug him before he disappeared. That was not good. Chicago was a scary enough place without crazy New Yorkers giving us ideas.

Mrs. Harker handed me the clipboard with the form still attached. I glanced at it and saw that she'd left a lot of blanks. Oh, well. I brought it back to the girl and she jumped up to take it from me, and then stuck her head around the corner.

"You can come in, Eva."

Before she went in Mrs. Harker gave me a nasty look, like all of this was somehow my fault. Then she pushed her brown cloth coat into my arms.

Laying the coat on the seat next to me, I settled down to read the rest of my newspaper. On the very last page of the city section there was a story about Vincent Renaldi's death. It didn't have many details: where he lived, worked and when he was thought to have died. At the very end of the article it said, "A suspect was detained but then released."

They'd let Appleton go. How could that happen? And how was there no mention of Rita Lindquist? Had they let her go, too? I had to get hold of Gardner. I lay the newspaper on the seat I'd been sitting in, dug through my pockets for the little notebook I carried; luckily there was a pen right next to it. I wrote a note for Mrs. Harker that said, "BE RIGHT BACK," ripped out the page and laid it on her coat. Then I rushed to the elevator and went up to the lobby. I found a bank of four pay phones in a hallway just off the main waiting room.

Looking up a number in the phone book, I had an eerie feeling about the telephone I was standing in front of. As though I could hear the conversations that had been had on it. "…not going to make it…died, he died…it's bad news… I'm sorry, I'm so sorry…" Shaking my head to chase away the voices, I dropped a quarter in and dialed Town Hall station. Honestly, though, I didn't expect the news I was about to receive would be much better.

It took almost five minutes for Gardner to come to the phone. When he did I said, "You let him go."

"Didn't have a choice."

"What happened?"

"Fucking lawyer showed up."

"So what. Appleton confessed."

"Yeah, right. According to his lawyer he's just trying to cover his girlfriend's ass." I got a sick feeling. I knew where this was going. "Called over to the coroner and asked a few questions. Only took five minutes to find some big ass problems in what Appleton'd been saying. Said he laced the cookies with anti-freeze, but the coroner says that wouldn't work. You'd just make someone sick. Says you'd have to use something else if you really wanted to kill someone. Something like rat poison."

"Did you arrest her?"

"What for?"

"Making a false report?"

"Can't prove that either. Not yet."

"What about the financial scam they're running? I told you I've got that nailed down."

Did I? I wasn't all that sure.

"Together? You can prove they're running it together?"

"I think so."

"I need more than you thinking so and you know it."

"When Appleton got the job she did the background check. He's a crook and she ignored it. Didn't tell Peterson-Palmer."

"Maybe she's just bad at her job? Maybe they should fire her."

"Her name—" I'd started to say her name was on the incorporation papers but it wasn't. The new registered agent was Rochelle LaRue. Quickly, I tried to think of a way that she was actually, concretely connected to the Ponzi scheme. But I couldn't.

"Don't worry. We'll get them," Gardner said.

"No. You won't."

I hung up and went back downstairs to Nuclear Medicine. Mrs. Harker was back in the waiting area, her coat on, my newspaper folded up on her lap beneath her black patent leather purse.

"You leave coat," she said when I got close.

"Oh, sorry."

"Someone could steal."

"Well, no one did, did they?" Though I did have to allow for the possibility that it *had* been stolen and she'd chased down the thief, beaten them, and taken back her coat.

"Hmmphf."

————

I SHOULD PROBABLY HAVE TAKEN Mrs. Harker to lunch somewhere and found a way to subtly prepare her for the next day's Christmas dinner. Instead, I took her back to her condo as quickly as possible. Rita and Bill were about to go underground, and I knew the only way I could pick up their trail would be to start right away.

From Edison Park, I drove back to Boystown and parked on Pine Grove right across the street from Rita's building. I didn't worry about her seeing the Versailles; I figured she wasn't there. And if she were maybe she'd come out and confront me if she saw the car. I pressed her number on the intercom system and waited for an answer. It didn't come, but that was okay. I had to at least pretend I was a normal person just there to visit a friend.

I walked around to the back of the building and looked

for a way in. There was a maze of three-story wooden porches clinging to the back of the building in a way that was uniquely Chicago. They'd put a wrought iron fence with a gate between the alley and the ten parking places that went with the building. There was a big green dumpster sitting on the outside of the fence. The people next door, though, used galvanized cans. I got one of those cans and set it next to the dumpster. Then I climbed up on top of the can, onto the dumpster, and lowered myself over the iron fence, careful not to impale myself.

I looked up at the back of Rita's building. Now I just had to figure out which condo was hers. I knew she was in 2F, which meant the second floor. F being the sixth letter of the alphabet told me that hers was probably the sixth back door on the second floor. There was a narrow walkway between buildings. I made my way down it trying to find the first back door.

The first floor was raised, but unlike a lot of buildings, the basement below didn't have garden apartments. It looked like it had laundry rooms and storage rooms instead. I looked up at the back doors on the first floor and was halfway down the walkway when I saw one that had 1C painted on. Not all of the apartments were numbered; probably the preference of the occupant. I walked toward the alley, blank, E, F and found that Rita's condo was on the second to last stairway.

I climbed up to the second floor. Her apartment was the one on the left. There was a back door and a large window that was barred. It was going to have to be the door. The door was wooden, without any kind of screen door, and had a glass window of about two foot by three foot.

I was about to do something very illegal and it deserved at least a second or two of consideration. I doubted that Rita gave breaking the law even those two seconds. And besides, I wasn't going to turn around and go home. Using my elbow, I broke the window.

A shard of glass managed to slice my trench coat, but didn't go all the way through to my arm. Lucky me. In addition to the very loud sound of glass crashing onto the floor, an alarm was going off. It wasn't a very loud alarm and it wasn't a "house" alarm. I reached through the broken window, felt around for the door knob, and pulled off one of those plastic boxes that hang from a door knob promising to deter burglars. I threw it off the back porch and it smashed to a thousand bits when it hit the concrete. So much for being deterred.

I stood there in the silence trying to determine if I'd caught anyone's attention. It was Christmas Eve and I doubted Rita's neighbors were at home. This was the kind of building young professionals would choose. Young professionals lived in distant states or came from the suburbs; what they didn't do was spend Christmas Eve home alone.

Reaching back through the window I opened the door, and carefully stepping over the broken glass, went inside. I shut the door behind me, not wanting things to look anymore out of the norm than they had to.

I was standing in Rita's kitchen. It was kind of an average kitchen, which pissed me off a little. She'd made at least two batches of poisoned cookies there in the last week. The room could have the courtesy to look a little sinister.

Then I stopped dead. Why hadn't the police been to search the apartment? This was where Bill lived as well. He'd briefly been their chief subject; wouldn't it have made sense to search the apartment? Of course, they might have had some trouble finding a judge on the Sunday before Christmas. And since they had to let Bill go, they might no longer have enough to get a search warrant. Either way, my being there was going to mess things up good if and when they got around to searching the place. Well, the damage was done. I might as well look around.

I went through a door and found myself in the dining room; also a bland, simple room with not much but a glass table and leather chairs. Through an arch the living room boasted a giant cream-colored sectional. There were a few random dresses thrown onto it. Beyond the living room was a sun porch with two uncomfortable looking metal and leather chairs. The furnishings were expensive but too sleek and modern to fit in this apartment.

To my left was the door to the bedroom. When I walked in it was hard to tell how the room was furnished since most of the clothing from the closet was tossed around the room. Presumably, Rita was traveling light. On the dresser, a jewelry box sat open. I poked through it. She'd taken the good stuff, if she had good stuff. I lifted the tray and looked underneath. There I found something interesting: passports, Illinois driver's licenses, credit cards.

There were two sets. One for Rita Lindquist and another for Rochelle LaRue. Rochelle LaRue lived at an address on Wilson Avenue in Uptown. My guess was it was a transient hotel, like the Hotel Chateau where I'd lived for a year. The kind of place that rented for five dollars a day and didn't ask a lot of questions. Rita probably rented a room for a week or two while she set up her new self. She'd stop by to pick up the mail. Once she collected everything she needed, she'd let the room go.

Thing was, she'd left all her paperwork for both Rita and Rochelle, and that meant something. It meant there was at least one more R.L. out there. The big question was, had she left Chicago or would she feel better hiding herself in a place she knew well.

She could hide herself in Chicago if she wanted to. There were places I didn't go to, places I'd never been. Some of them were places that Rita, and Bill presumably, would stick out like a sore thumb. Black neighborhoods, Mexican neighborhoods. But there were a lot of other neighborhoods where they could go unnoticed, particularly if they went to a thrift shop and made themselves look poor and desperate. People went to extra trouble to ignore the poor and desperate.

So, how was I going to figure out Rita's new identity? I wandered around her apartment for a few more minutes and then decided to leave. For the moment, I was stumped.

Chapter Fourteen

ABOUT AN INCH of snow had collected over the city, which had me hoping it wouldn't be all brown and slushy for Christmas Day. Chicago and snow plus Christmas equaled automatic joy, a restoration of all that was right and good. None of that was true, of course. It had all the phoniness of a corny Christmas card—but I still wished for it.

I grabbed a gyros and fries from a place on Belmont, and went back to my office. Despite the cold, I hoped to be sitting at my desk unwrapping my lunch while it was still vaguely warm. It was not to be.

Standing in front of my door, wrapped in her black fur coat, looking like a magazine ad, was Gloria Silver.

"There you are," she said, as though we had an appointment and I was late.

"What do you want?"

"You could be a little friendlier."

"You've hated me since the moment we met and now I find out you've had a private investigator tailing me for God knows how long, and you expect me to be friendly?"

"Invite me into your office, it's freezing in this hallway."

I doubted she was even chilled. Given the coat she wore, she could have spent a weekend tobogganing with Dr. Zhivago and not felt the cold. Against my better judgment, I opened the door and let her in.

My office is a misshapen room with a terrible carpet and worse furniture. Gloria took one look and said, "I have to congratulate you. This is every bit as awful as I expected."

"Believe it or not, it keeps the riff-raff out." And by riff-raff I meant people like Gloria Silver.

She sat down in my guest chair and opened her coat in such a way that it was the only thing in the room she actually touched. "I'd like to hire you."

"No."

"I can't blame you for that, I suppose. I'll pay twenty percent above your regular fee."

"You can double my fee and I wouldn't work for you."

"I want you to find Rita Lindquist. Don't you want to find her?"

"I'm going to find her." How escaped me at the moment but I would.

"Why don't you let me pay your fee then, since you're going to do what I want anyway."

I noticed she dropped the twenty percent extra. Since I had no intention of working for her, I didn't bother to haggle. On the other hand, if she thought she was going to be my client she might answer a few questions. And I did have questions.

"I saw you with Rita and Bill at the 95th. You all looked friendly enough."

Gloria brushed that off with a shrug. "And then Rita told the state's attorney the most dreadful pack of lies."

"And you know that because...?"

"I was interviewed this morning. Merry Christmas to me, right?"

"You know you might be better off if Rita never comes back."

"Really? I hadn't thought about it that way." There was a distinct lack of sincerity in her voice. She'd thought about it that way, all right.

"Were you involved in the Ponzi scheme she and Bill had going?"

"I wouldn't call it a Ponzi scheme exactly."

"In other words, yes. Has she left you holding the bag?"

"She tried to make it seem like it was all my idea. Really, I'm not that clever." Really, I suspected she was.

"Is that what you told the state's attorney? That you're not very bright?"

"There's no reason to be insulting."

"Did you know Bill Appleton before Rita met him?"

"I may have suggested he apply at Peterson-Palmer. I certainly had no idea they'd hit it off the way they did." There was a note of jealousy in her voice. I wondered if losing men to other women—or for that matter other men—was a common occurrence for Gloria.

"You've been throwing a lot of money around. That's going to make you look kind of guilty."

"Yes, that *is* a problem. But you see, I didn't get that money from Bill and Rita." She paused; she didn't want to say what came next but she didn't have much choice. "I may have, on occasion, taken tips for not mentioning certain things I know in my column."

"Did you tell that to the state's attorney?"

"It slipped my mind."

"Because of its resemblance to blackmail?"

"That's such a vulgar way of putting things."

"Most of the law is vulgar when you get down to it. Did Rita uncover those certain things for you?"

"I'm not sure. I don't remember every source."

"And you're a journalist so you don't reveal your sources anyway."

"Why, yes…" Clearly, that hadn't crossed her mind. At least, I knew what she'd be saying next time she talked to the state's attorney.

"Of course, if a source reveals you there's not much you can do about it, is there?" I said.

"Won't you help me? Please?"

"You opened Pandora's Box. Now you want me to close it."

"Look at this however you like, just please help me."

"No."

"What are you going to do with Rita when you find her?"

"Turn her over to the police."

"That seems, I don't know, anti-climactic."

"What do you think I should do with her?"

"You did say I'd be better off if she didn't come back. Wouldn't you be better off, too?"

I burst out laughing. Couldn't help myself. "Are you trying to hire me to kill Rita Lindquist?"

"Don't act so surprised. You do work for Jimmy English, after all."

"I used to work for Jimmy's lawyer. That's different."

"I don't see how."

"No, you wouldn't."

———

UNABLE TO SECURE my services as a hit man, Gloria issued a few vile threats and left. I was tempted to call Sugar and tell her about the encounter, but I couldn't get over the nagging feeling that Rita and Bill were slipping away. I had to find them.

But that was going to be difficult since the city was shutting down for the holiday. Of course, they were up against the same problems I was. If they were trying to leave the city by air, they were facing huge crowds and trouble getting tickets—especially if it mattered to them where they were going. They might be willing to leave by bus or train, but could be facing the same obstacles—not to mention they'd been traveling by limo just yesterday. A bus or train might not suit.

The easiest way to leave the city was by car. The problem there would be whose car. They wouldn't want anything registered to either Rita Lindquist or Bill Appleton, so I wondered did they have a vehicle registered under a different name?

I decided to eat my now very cold gyros and make a list of things I needed to do after the holiday.

Number one. I could follow through on my original plan and bring the packet I'd put together down to the state's attorney's office. Logically, I knew the best way to find Rita and Bill would be to let the state do it. They did have more resources than I did. Which didn't mean I still wouldn't love to do it myself.

Number two. One of the best ways to find someone was to find their money. I hadn't seen any bank statements when I was in Rita's condo. I should have looked harder. Of course, Bill might have an account at Peterson-Palmer. So might Rita. If they were smart they'd have put their ill-gotten gains right into an account that might make them some legally gotten gains. And they'd have wanted to do that somewhere they could keep a close eye on it. Not to mention, Bill could open the accounts himself so no one would look too closely at whatever I.D. they used.

I had an idea that Raymond might be able to get his hands on their accounts—provided they did actually have money at Peterson-Palmer. Hopefully whatever went on in the conference room after I left was good enough that Raymond would want to help me. I made him my second stop on Wednesday.

Number three. Williams Hanover and its various shell corporations. I needed to do more digging when it came to those companies. Were any of the agents or board members real people? And were any of those real people able to tell me where Rita and Bill had gone to?

Number four. I had to figure out what names they were using. Rita appeared to be a pro at setting up new identities for herself. It wouldn't be difficult for her to do the same for Bill. Something suddenly hit me and I stopped taking notes. I slipped my trench coat back on and dashed out of the office. There was someone I wanted to talk to who might actually still be around.

I zigzagged my way across the snow-covered sidewalks of Boystown until I reached Cornelia and Lake Shore Drive. Hurrying past the building's doorman a second time, I took the elevator up to the twelfth floor and was knocking on Doreen Appleton's door moments later. As I waited there, I worried she was already off with relatives somewhere and I was wasting my time—but then the door opened.

Doreen wore a pair of tight, black ski pants and a bulky white sweater. Her hair was pulled into a giant pigtail with a thick pink tie. Behind her on the couch was an open suitcase, half full of warm clothing, a form-fitting parka and a pair of shiny snow skis.

"Oh, it's Mr. Broken Heart," she said.

"You saw right through me."

"People lie to you enough eventually you catch on."

"Can I come in for a minute?"

"I'm a little pressed for time."

"It won't take long."

She stepped back and let me in. After she closed the door, she asked, "So, who are you really?"

"I'm a private investigator, Nick Nowak."

I offered her my card. She took it and looked it over.

"Who are you working for?"

"Peterson-Palmer."

"So you work with Bill and Rita?"

"Not exactly. I work for Vincent Renaldi."

"Who's that?"

"Doesn't matter. He's dead."

That seemed to take the stuffing out of her. She picked up a pair of jeans, folded them and put them into her suitcase. "I'm going to Aspen for Christmas. I have a flight in about two hours. That's what divorced people do for the holidays. We go skiing."

"Don't you want to know who killed Vincent Renaldi?"

"I don't think I'm going to like the answer."

"Bill confessed to the murder yesterday."

"So he's in jail."

"No, he wasn't telling the truth."

"You mean, he didn't kill this Renaldi guy? Why'd he tell the police he did?"

"He and Rita killed Vincent. Together. They just went to the police and told them enough lies to make it hard to figure out what really happened."

"But they'll figure it out eventually."

"Maybe, maybe not. In the meantime, all the evidence is tainted and there's nothing left to arrest them on. Poof. Bill and Rita disappear."

"Oh," Doreen said. It was a small, flat little word. It was also the sound of her future disappearing. I had the feeling her divorce was paying for the ski trip and she'd planned on it paying for a lot more. But no Bill, no alimony. No big monetary settlement.

Of course, it would probably be a lot worse than that for her. Once the Ponzi scheme was exposed people were going to want any money Bill gave her. If you marry a car thief you don't get to keep the Caddy he stole for your birthday when he gets caught. She'd probably lose her savings, and her condo to boot. I decided to keep that information to myself, though. Why ruin her holiday?

"Do you know Gloria Silver?" I asked.

"The gossip columnist? No, I don't know her. What does she have to do with this?" Her voice was getting clipped and a little angry.

"Does Bill know her?"

"Yeah, he does. He's from Naperville. He grew up across the street from the Silvers. Used to mow their lawn when he'd come home from college. She helped him get on at Peterson-Palmer after he was fired from BFO."

"BFO?"

"Becker, Fleet and O'Day. I'm not feeling well. I need a glass of water."

She walked out of the living room into a small galley kitchen. I took out the little notebook I always carried. When she came back she had glass of water in her hand. The glass had Santa Claus painted on it.

"Why was he fired from Becker, Fleet and O'Day?"

"He said he'd made a simple mistake that anyone could make and he'd been fired for it. We were still married then and in love. I believed him."

"And your lawyer found out differently?"

"Yeah, Bill tried to get everyone over sixty to let him manage their accounts. I actually thought that's what financial planners did, but I guess they're really only supposed to give advice."

"Do you know any of these names?" I asked, and then

read off my little notebook. "Myron Shaver, Walter Seyd, or Martin Goewy?"

"Walter Seyd was my great uncle. He gave me away at our wedding."

"Was?"

"He passed away three years ago." Which meant he wasn't using his identity. I wondered if Bill was traveling under that name now?

"And you don't know Myron Shaver or Martin Goewy."

"Bill might have had a cousin Marty. I don't really remember."

"A dead cousin?"

"Yeah."

"Thanks, that helps."

"You're going to try to find him?"

"I'm going to find him."

———

IT WAS GETTING late and I'd done as much as I could. I had a couple of names that Bill Appleton might be traveling under and that was a start. It might not get me anywhere, but it could help the state's attorney or the FBI or whoever's lap this all landed in. And I guess I was going to have to be happy about that.

As I walked along Lake Shore Drive heading home, the night was frigid and clear. The temperature had to be well under freezing. My breath was forming little icicles on my mustache. The day's snow was turning crisp and brittle. I hoped it warmed a little and snowed again for Christmas—

Shit. I hadn't bought Joseph a gift. Any gift. Or Mrs. Harker. Or anyone, for that matter. None of that had crossed my mind since Vincent was killed. I suppose I had a good excuse. In fact, I probably had a couple of good excuses, but that didn't make it feel any better.

When I walked into the apartment, Joseph was dressed in jeans, a pressed white shirt, a navy jacket and penny loafers. An overcoat was thrown onto one of the director's chairs.

"Glad you're here," he said. "I just left a message at your office."

"What's going on?"

"I told you, I promised to drop by my parents on Christmas Eve."

"Oh, I forgot."

"It's okay. My sister called. Now my parents do want me to come tomorrow, but I said no. Tonight's all they get."

"Okay. Where's Ross?" The couch was empty.

"Brian came and got him. They were supposed to do something with Franklin's friends, but Brian put his foot down and said he wanted to spend Christmas Eve with Ross."

"Just the three of them?"

"You're invited."

"Sounds dreamy."

"You could come with me. I mean, you'd have to be my roommate."

"One of your roommates. Don't forget you have two."

"And an imaginary apartment much bigger than this one."

"I think I'll stay here. Watch *Miracle on 34th Street* again."

"You're just a big softy." Then he kissed me, sweetly, romantically. He pulled me to him.

"I love you, Nick."

"I love you, too."

Chapter Fifteen

"COME ON, TIME TO GET UP," Joseph whispered in my ear. "It's Christmas."

"Ten more minutes."

"Nope, Ross wants to open his presents."

"Oh shit. I didn't get anyone anything."

"Yeah, you did."

And with that he bounced off the bed. He'd piqued my curiosity, so I rolled out of bed and walked out into the living room. Someone had turned on WGN and the Yule log was burning on the TV. Ross was back sitting on the couch under a blanket. There was a pile of wrapped gifts on the sofa next to him.

"Good morning," he said.

"Hey," I glanced out the window, the sun was rising and the sky was clear. Everything looked cold and brittle.

"Do we know how cold it is out?"

"I had the news on for a while. They said one degree."

I gave an involuntary shiver. "How was Brian's?"

"It was good. He and Franklin compromised. Two of

Franklin's best friends came down for an hour or so. They were okay."

"Really?"

"The girl kept going to the bathroom to wash her hands. Probably my fault."

"You have that effect on people," I said before I really thought it through. But it was okay. He laughed. He was good with gallows humor.

Joseph handed me a hot cup of coffee. "Oh, thank you." I took a sip and then looked around for my cigarettes. They were on the table next to the ashtray. "How about you, Joseph? How was your evening?"

"My parents think you're a woman."

"Was it something I said?"

"That's the only logical reason they can think of for me to leave the priesthood."

"They're going to be very disappointed," Ross said.

"I'm not wearing a dress for you," I told Joseph.

"Oh God, what a horrible thought," Ross said, his face a mask of terror. Then he quickly shifted gears. "Come on, I want to open presents."

He picked out two gifts from the pile and offered them to Joseph and me. We sat down in the director's chairs. I set my coffee on the floor thinking that maybe I should get an end table. My package was small, while Joseph's was much larger. Each was carefully wrapped in Santa Claus-themed paper.

"You first," I said to Joseph.

He unwrapped his present to find a nice box about an inch deep and a bit bigger than a letter-sized piece of paper. He pulled off the lid and inside was a leather portfolio with a place for a pad of paper and a gold-plated pen in a holder on the spine.

"It's for taking notes at school," Ross said.

"I see that."

Now I knew why Brian had steered me away from school supplies. He'd probably taken Ross shopping before he went with me.

"It's great. Thank you Ross," Joseph said.

Then they looked at me. It was my turn. Quickly, I opened my present. It was a silver cigarette case with a brown alligator skin inlay. I opened I up and saw that it was inscribed, "All my love, Helen."

I gave Ross a look.

"It's from a thrift store."

"It's very cool."

"I thought about having someone scratch out Helen and put Ross, but I kind of liked the idea of there being some woman somewhere named Helen who pines after an old flame and dreams of what might have been if he hadn't been a depraved homosexual."

"Why do I have the feeling the whole reason to buy the gift was to call me a depraved homosexual."

"Because it was?" Ross said.

"All right, here are my gifts," Joseph said. From the sofa, he picked out two packages wrapped in gold paper and decorated with red ribbon. Handed one to me and one to Ross. I let Ross open his first. Inside his package were two paperback novels, both by Stephen King: *Carrie* and *Salem's Lot*.

In answer to a very obvious question, Joseph said, "You watch too much TV."

"So you thought you'd scare me into reading?"

"They're good, you'll like them."

"Wait a minute. A priest who likes Stephen King? Did you quit or did they throw you out?"

My gift was relatively obvious since it was a thin square, twelve inches on each side. It was an album or two. The only surprise was going to be who the artist was. I was really hoping it wasn't Michael Jackson.

When I peeled off the paper, I found three Keith Jarrett albums: *Expectations*, an older album I did not have, which meant he'd actually gone through my records deciding what I'd like; and *Standards, Volume 1* and *Standards, Volume 2*. He'd done very well—especially for someone whose musical tastes were decidedly mainstream.

I kissed Joseph on the cheek and said, "You did good."

"I'm glad."

"This one's for you from Brian," Ross said, handing me an oblong box wrapped in shiny red paper. It was pretty obvious what it was, but I didn't say anything until I opened the box and found the expected bottle of Johnnie Walker Red.

"You'll tell Brian I acted shocked?"

"Of course."

"I'm sorry I didn't get you guys anything," I said. "It's been kind of busy."

"But you did get us something," Joseph said, picking up the last two boxes. He handed one box to Ross and kept one for himself.

"Well, I can't wait to see what I got you."

Ross opened his first. "Slippers!" It was a nice pair of corduroy slippers with flannel linings. They went right onto Ross' bare feet.

"And can you believe it?" Joseph asked. "I got slippers, too." He'd opened an almost identical pair. "Thank you, Nick."

"Okay, we're not going to pretend I bought those."

"No, we're not," said Joseph. "And we're also not going to pretend I didn't steal the money out of your wallet to buy them."

I was dying for a cigarette. Most of the time I tried to

smoke over by the window so I could crack it a little. But the fact that it was one degree outside made that a bit unappealing. Impulsively, I said, "I know what I'll give you for Christmas." I held my Marlboros.

"Nick, I don't want your cigarettes."

"No, take them. Throw them away. I'm done. I quit. That's your Christmas present."

"Really."

"Yeah, really." I was regretting it already. But it was done.

"Nick, that's the best present ever," Joseph said, before he threw his arms around me.

———

ON MY WAY out to pick up Mrs. Harker, I drove past a branch of Midtown Bank and the clock spelled out ten degrees in orange bulbs. If she was standing outside when I got there I was going to kill her. Well, I probably wasn't going to actually kill her. That wouldn't be very Christmassy. But I was definitely going to be pissed.

It was nearly eleven and I hadn't had a cigarette all morning. For the first time, I noticed that the car smelled like cigarette smoke. Which made sense since there were cigarette butts in the ashtray. It's just that when you smoke, one of the things you don't smell is cigarette smoke. Unfortunately, the smell of the car just made me desperate to light up.

I pulled up to the Harker condo and Mrs. Harker was not standing on the curb. Thank God. She was standing in the lobby, which, while not as warm as her condo, was not ten degrees. She and Terry came out and got into the car. She carried a large platter of Christmas cookies covered in Saran Wrap. Her black purse dangled from her wrist. On the lapel of her brown cloth coat she'd pinned an enamel angel. She'd even been somewhere and had her hair done.

I looked into the back seat and said to Terry, "You could have carried the cookies for her."

"Like she'd let me."

"Is true. Boy drop."

"I wouldn't drop them. I can carry things."

"Boy drop strawberry jam. All over floor."

"Oh my God! That was three months ago."

"Floor still sticky."

"It is not."

"In corner."

"Oh my God."

Believe it or not, I think she was teasing Terry. I wondered if this was how they spent most of their time together. He wore new-ish jeans, a down jacket and what looked like a dress shirt underneath. Usually, his fashion choices were more outlandish. My guess was she'd teased him into dressing a little more conservatively.

I pulled away from the curb. I needed to at least prepare her a little for what she was facing and I thought she might hesitate to jump out of a moving car.

"There are going to be five of us for dinner. Two of my friends will be there."

"I know. Your friend, Brian."

"Well, no, Brian is having Christmas with his boyfriend, Franklin."

"Who is Joseph?" she asked, throwing me.

"Um, I live with him."

"She was worried you were cooking," Terry said from the back seat. "I told her Joseph would probably be the one cooking. She has a sandwich in her purse in case dinner sucks."

"Hush," she snapped at him. "Is very silly boy."

Of course, that didn't mean she didn't have a sandwich in her purse.

"And my friend Ross is going to be there. He's been staying with us. Because he needs a place to stay."

She shrugged.

I glanced down at the platter of cookies in her lap. It looked like there were half a dozen kinds on the platter. Intricate, careful cookies in the shape of stars and hearts and Christmas trees, dusted with powdered sugar and covered in plastic wrap. She may have spent as much time as she would have on dinner.

"The cookies look wonderful."

"Is not big thing."

But I think it probably was.

We fell into a companionable silence the rest of the way. I knew that my 'preparations' had not been close to adequate, but I was hoping for a Christmas miracle.

Pulling up in front of Two Towers, the fifteen-story brick building loomed over us. Not surprisingly, there were two towers and a sort of lobby/hallway that spanned between them. There was a circular drive that I used to drop off Mrs. Harker and Terry before I drove off to look for a parking space. I gave Terry a very serious look and said, "Wait for me." I didn't want him taking Mrs. Harker up to the tenth floor without me.

It took ten minutes to find a parking space of questionable legality on Broadway. I really hoped meter maids got Christmas off. Walking to my apartment, I was a little buzzed. Lots of things were making me nervous, not the least of which was the complete lack of nicotine in my system. I was also worried that Rita and Bill were managing to leave Chicago while I exchanged gifts with my friends. And then, of course, there was the time bomb waiting in my lobby: Mrs. Harker.

Terry had been a good boy and kept her there with him. They stood near the empty desk in the middle, the one that a doorman might have sat at if they ever decided to pay for one. Mrs. Harker still held the cookies even though she could have set them down. I might have said something to Terry about it, but he was right, she probably wouldn't let him hold them or even set them onto the desk. I smiled at them, flipped down the collar of my trench coat, and led them to the elevator.

When we walked into the apartment, the first thing Mrs. Harker noticed was the view. "Is nice—"

She stopped and stared at Ross sitting on the sofa. He was dressed, which was unusual, wearing just a pair of jeans, a plaid shirt, his waiter's black bow tie and the slippers Joseph had given him. He was obviously sick. Above his collar were the purple Karposi lesions. I was so used to them it was like I'd stopped seeing them.

Mrs. Harker's eyes filled with tears. I hadn't thought this through—I'd been worried that Joseph would be the problem. I hadn't thought about the emaciated man dying far too soon on the same sofa where her emaciated son had spent months dying far too soon. Ross reminded her of Harker. Of course he would.

"This is my friend, Ross," I said, hoping to break the spell. "And this is Joseph."

She looked at Joseph, recognition and surprise filling her face.

"Hello, Eva, nice to see you again. The cookies look wonderful. They haven't been out of your sight, have they?" he joked.

Mrs. Harker looked at him like he was insane. Then her face set into a frown. She was putting things together, understanding who was who. And what was what. She shoved the platter of cookies at Joseph then went into my bedroom and slammed the door.

Joseph and I stared at each other until I said, "Well, that went much better than I expected."

"You're kidding, right?" Ross asked.

"Oh no. I expected her to run from the apartment screaming. That she ran into the bedroom is a good sign. Why don't you all have a cookie? She's a very good cook. I suspect they're delicious."

I went to the bedroom door; I knocked and said, "Mrs. Harker?" then let myself in. She sat on the edge of my bed— which Joseph had carefully made—her arms tightly crossed. Anger and sadness flashing across her face like a storm. I sat next to her.

"My world is gone," she said. "I don't know this world."

One of the advantages of dying young, I thought. *Never losing one's world.*

"Bert would be glad you're here. With people who care about you."

"Father Joseph is here," she said as though it might be a shock to me. "They say things at church. Terrible things. *True* things."

"Joseph left the church and now he lives here with me."

For a moment I saw a flash of the old, unforgiving Mrs. Harker as she said, "You steal from God."

"It's only fair. God steals from us."

She thought about that and then she made a noise that was distantly related to a chuckle.

"We should not be mad at God."

"I think he can take it."

After one final suspicious, angry look, she deflated. It was a horrible thing to watch. I'd come to respect her bluster, her anger, her rigidity, her stubbornness. As much as I would have liked her to enjoy the day, I hated seeing her simply give up.

"Would you like an easy pill?"

"Yes. And a whiskey."

Having planned ahead, I had the pills in my coat pocket. I took out a pill and broke it in half. I didn't want to give her a whole one if she was going to have whiskey. She swallowed it down without water.

I took off my trench coat and laid it on the bed. She hadn't moved. "Mrs. Harker, stand up and take off you coat." She did as she was told. Underneath the coat, she wore a dark blue suit with a light blue blouse.

"You look very nice."

She snorted. That was a good sign.

We went back out into the living room. I poured Mrs. Harker some Johnnie Walker. No ice, no water. "Just put in glass," she'd instructed.

Joseph made mimosas for everyone else. It was still before noon, after all. He asked Terry to turn on the stereo and made a tray of cheese and crackers. Bing Crosby began to sing "Silent Night." That killed conversation for about three minutes.

Then there wasn't any place to put the cheese and crackers because the table was too small for the bowl of ornaments, the platter of cookies and the appetizers. Terry put the ornaments on the windowsill, while Joseph moved the cookies to the bookshelf—but not before handing a cookie out to everyone.

"The cookies are wonderful, Eva," he said. And they were wonderful.

"They're great," added Ross.

"You went to a lot of trouble," noted Joseph.

"Is not big thing."

"How is Father Dewes? It's been months since I've talked to him."

"He has flu," she said somewhat uncertainly. She came from a generation that idolized their priests. They weren't fallible human beings, they were God's emissaries. I'm sure admitting that he was ill felt like a betrayal.

We ate dinner a little after noon. Joseph had made the smallest turkey he could find—about nine pounds, mashed potatoes, oyster stuffing from canned oysters, green beans, biscuits that had to be cooked after the turkey came out and it was cooling, gravy, and cranberry sauce from a can.

The five of us squeezed around the tiny dining table that barely sat four. The food was set out on the stove and on the six-inch marble windowsill that ran the length of the living room window.

Before we began, Joseph said grace. "Dear God, on this joyful day radiant with the brilliance of Your true love, may Your love fill our hearts and our lives. Bless us and the feast that You have provided for us. Let us be thankful for the true gift of Christmas, Your unquestioning love. Amen."

Mrs. Harker studied him as he encouraged everyone to start passing around the food. God's love was only unquestioning in a few parts of the New Testament. Everywhere else, his love was a whole lot of questions that doomed you to hell if you answered wrong.

Terry turned the record over and the Andrews Sisters joined Bing for a bouncy version of "Jingle Bells." Joseph tried to engage Mrs. Harker in conversation. "What was Chicago like when you first came?"

She didn't want to play, though, and all she'd say was, "Different. Better."

"Yes, it does sometimes seem like the world gets worse every year. But then, some things do get better."

Mrs. Harker didn't reply. To be fair, the Valium might have kicked in, making conversation a challenge.

Terry and Ross complimented Joseph on the food—and they were right to, Joseph had done a good job. That led to a long discussion of the kinds of holiday meals we had as kids.

Toward the end of that discussion, "Christmas in Killarney" came on and Joseph said, "This one's my mother's favorite."

And then we were finished. Terry immediately asked if he could use the phone to call his friend Cherry. When I said yes, he dragged the phone into the bathroom and shut the door. Given that I only had one bathroom that might eventually be a problem. Ross went back over to the sofa and pulled a blanket over his lap. I could tell that the day was exhausting him. He'd eaten a lot, though, and that had a to be a good thing. I tried not to think about how much I wanted a cigarette with my coffee.

While picking up the dishes, Joseph whispered into my ear, "Present." I followed his eyes over to the sofa and there, sitting next to Ross, was one more nicely wrapped present. I walked over and took a look at it and saw that it was for Mrs. Harker from me.

I took it across the room and handed it to her. "Merry Christmas, Mrs. Harker."

Calmly, a bit too calmly, she opened the box. Slippers. Joseph must have run across a really good sale.

"Thank you," she said. Then went back to looking out the window again. The whiskey and the Valium had not been a good idea. Not together. She looked as though she wanted to take a very long nap.

I stepped over to Joseph who standing at the Pullman kitchen dealing with the remains of dinner. "Can you make a plate for Mrs. Harker? I think I should take her home."

"That might be a good idea," he agreed.

I went to the bedroom, put my coat on, and grabbed Mrs. Harker's. I stood there thinking for a moment, deciding, and then I grabbed a shoebox from the top of my closet. I tucked the box under my arm and went back out into the living room.

Opening up her coat, I told Mrs. Harker, "I think it's

time I took you home." Docilely, she stood up and slipped her arms into the coat.

From the couch, Ross said, "It was very nice to meet you, Mrs. Harker."

"Yes," she managed.

At the door, Joseph handed her a plate of leftovers, then adjusted her collar, telling her, "It was very nice seeing you, Eva. I hope we'll be seeing a lot of each other."

She flashed him a horrified look and I knew that I hadn't overdosed her. Then she asked, "What about boy?"

"Didn't he tell you? He's staying at Brian's tonight."

She looked confused for a moment, then said, "Oh, yes, he tell me."

I pounded on the bathroom door. "Terry, say goodbye to Mrs. Harker."

"Good-bye, Mrs. Harker," he shouted through the bathroom door.

I rolled my eyes and we left the apartment.

Chapter Sixteen

"THE SLIPPERS ARE FROM JOSEPH," I said as I pulled up in front of the Harker condo. "I got too busy to get you anything."

"Is fine. I have many slippers."

I didn't know what she meant exactly, so I just continued. "I did think of something else I could share with you. If I can come in for a bit."

She glanced at me suspiciously and sighed heavily, but said, "Is okay." Then she got out of the car. I pulled into a parking spot, got the shoebox out of the backseat, and followed her into the condo.

Inside, I took off my soggy shoes and draped the trench coat over one of her dining room chairs. I'd been in the condo many times and I still found it odd that Harker had ever lived there. I knew he had, but it wasn't as though he'd invited me over while we were dating. So I didn't know how he'd walk around the rooms, how'd hold himself, where he'd sit.

I had trouble connecting him to the place. That meant the two-bedroom, modestly furnished condo was all Mrs.

Harker. It was always ridiculously neat with the stale smell of cooking in the air. And not the stale smell of Christmas cookies. No, it was always something made with cabbage.

We sat at the dining room table. Almost immediately, she got up, went into the kitchen, and returned with a pressed tin ashtray from a drawer. This was an honor. She'd never allowed me to smoke in the condo. I must have been doing something right.

"I quit. This morning. It was my Christmas gift to Joseph."

That earned a sour look. Not that I'd quit smoking, I think she hated the cigarettes. But I think giving it up for the boyfriend I'd stolen from the priesthood hit a nerve. She left the ashtray there like a dare. I decided not to revisit the subject of Joseph. We could save that for another time.

I opened the shoebox. Inside were about two dozen microcassettes and a small recorder to play them on. The cassettes had belonged to Christian Baylor. The recorder was mine, though he'd used the same model to make the tapes. Harker had given it to him.

The cassettes were identified only by date. Interviews he'd done beginning in mid-1982 to early 1984 right before his death. The ones I wanted were from August and September of 1982. I put the earliest cassette in. It was dated 9/7/82.

Christian came on and said, "Bughouse Slasher Interviews." September seventh. This is Christian Baylor."

There was a long dramatic pause. Mrs. Harker watched me nervously.

"So, why do you keep looking for him?" we heard Christian ask. "You're retired. Why can't you let the CPD take it over?"

Bert replied, "Because we can't forget about them. They were just boys. Not very nice boys maybe, but still just boys."

Mrs. Harker's hand flew up to cover her mouth. "Is

Bertram," she said in a small, child-like voice.

"Yes," I said.

Bert continued. "He took away their right to grow, to become better, to become men. He took away their right to decide what their stories would be. No one should do that, no one should decide for you."

"No, they should not," Mrs. Harker said, as though he was there and they were talking.

On the tape, Christian asked, "And you think the CPD will just forget about them?

"Yes, I do think that. The boys were all gay. Most officers think they got what they deserved."

"Was it hard for you, being a gay cop?"

"Yes. Very. It was hardest at first. You see I believed all the things everyone else believed. That there was something wrong with me. That I was disgusting. That I needed to be fixed."

A tear ran down Mrs. Harker's face.

"Do you want to stop?" I asked.

She shook her head.

"…the real conflict was inside of me. I even went to a psychiatrist for a while, but he only intensified those feelings. But then, eventually, I began to think that the problem might not be me. That maybe I wasn't the one who was wrong. Things started getting better after that. I mean, I still wasn't out, but I did know that when people said cruel things, they were wrong."

"That didn't make it harder not to challenge them?"

Bert gave that some thought. "Well, no, I don't think so. When you become a cop you want to make the world a better place. But you learn, you learn very quickly, that you can't. You can make some small things better, you can right a wrong here and there, but the world is what it is. You can't fix it all."

"I'd like to go back over the cases, if you don't mind."

"I don't mind at all. I go back over them all the time." After a moment, he began. "The first murder was in October of 1980. We thought it was nothing special, most murders are about greed or romance gone wrong. That was what we thought it was. The boy had a friend who reported him missing. He wouldn't say it at first, but they'd been boyfriends. We thought the motive was jealousy."

Harker continued for a long time. Not all of the cases were his. At first. Eventually, though they became his as he put together the Slasher's pattern. As he learned what the Slasher liked.

After he talked about each of the other cases, Christian asked, "Do you think he'll ever be caught?"

"I know he'll be caught."

"How can you be sure?"

"I'm going to catch him."

That was where the tape ended. I cleared my throat. Mrs. Harker wiped tears off her cheeks. I spent a moment or two trying to remember what Christian had said to me when I asked if he'd known what Harker was up to but I couldn't remember.

And then I thought, *They're both dead. It doesn't matter.* It didn't really. I knew what happened. If Christian knew what might happen beforehand, well, that was something he'd had to live with.

"Bert was a good man," I said. "You made a good man."

"Yes. He was good man."

She put her gnarled hand on top of mine. "Did you kill him? Did you kill the bad man?"

Almost a year before she'd asked the same question. I lied to her then. I couldn't lie to her now.

"Yes. I killed him."

"Thank you."

————

WHEN I GOT HOME, we were having a party. Or rather, it felt like a party. The apartment was small enough that you didn't need many people for it to feel like a crowd. Brian and Franklin had stopped by with an entire box of leftovers and two bottles of champagne. I didn't own anything resembling champagne flutes, so we drank from the teacups that came with my cheap set of dishes. Someone had lit candles.

Joseph handed me a cup of champagne the moment I stepped through the door. Then he got busy heating up the leftovers. It seemed we were going to have a second holiday meal. I stared at the champagne a bit horrified. How was I going to have a drink without a cigarette? For the fiftieth time that day I kicked myself for not getting Joseph a plain old boring Christmas gift. There was nothing wrong with pair of pajamas, a bottle of cologne or even a bar of soap stuck to a goddamn rope. Why was none of that good enough for me? Yes, it would not have stacked up well next to the jazz albums Joseph got me. But then Joseph would have had the pleasure of being the better, more thoughtful person. I didn't want to be the better person. I wanted a cigarette.

Brian came over and asked, "Are you okay?"

"Yeah, I'm fine," I took a sip of champagne. It tasted lonely.

"Where's Terry?"

"I gave him cab fare to go to his friend Cherry's house."

"Do you think he's really—"

"I talked to Cherry's mother. He's probably going to spend the night."

"Oh, good," I said. He was an emancipated minor, which meant we made sure he was housed and fed and not getting into trouble. Of course, we weren't parents, so there wasn't much we could do if he did decide to get into trouble.

"Sugar asked me to be her man-of-honor at the wedding."

"That's happening?"

"Yes. She's really excited," he said, clearly confused by my tone. I have to admit I was surprised she still planned to marry Michael France. Since Brian was there when Sugar asked me to look into her fiancé, I supposed it might be okay to talk to him about what I'd found out.

On the other hand, it felt like a big violation of her privacy. I decided to be careful with what I said. "I found some things out about Michael. Things that—"

"She told me," Brian said.

"She did? What did he say?"

"That Michael got into to some trouble when he was in art school."

That sounded like he was involved in some kind of fraternity prank, but I let it go. It was certainly up to Sugar how truthful she wanted to be.

"And the thing with Gloria, " I said.

"About the house? Yeah, Sugar said Michael's paying her back." I assumed the money he'd be using would be Sugar's.

"Gloria's gonna need the money. I think she has some sticky legal issues coming up."

"Really?

I said a few very general things about the Ponzi scheme. I didn't want to say too much. Not just because of confidentiality issues, but also I wasn't entirely sure I understood everything. For example, I wasn't all that sure the mutual funds even existed. A computer wouldn't actually check to see if a fund was real, would it? Someone could just put in information and it would look real just by virtue of being there.

Ross turned the television on and said, "Oh my God! I love this movie."

Channel 9 was playing *Christmas in Connecticut* with Barbara Stanwyck.

"I can't believe the paper only gave it two stars." Ross said, as he adjusted the rabbit ears.

"Must have been reviewed by a woman," Franklin said.

"What do you mean?"

"Well, the big joke is that Barbara Stanwyck's character is a woman who can't do woman's work."

"Maybe I don't see it that way; maybe I see it as a person who can't take care of herself and then she learns to," Ross replied.

"By taking care of a man."

"Thank you, Gloria Steinem."

"It's Mrs. Harker's generation," I pointed out. "Things were different then."

The movie began and Franklin's attempts to continue to make his point were shushed. Ross and Brian settled on the sofa to watch the movie. I went over and sat at the little table, which was only a foot or two from the kitchen.

Joseph said, "Somebody in Franklin's family is a really good cook."

From the other side of the room, Franklin said, "My mother."

Ross and Brian shushed him again.

Quietly, Joseph said to me, "Eva did pretty well, don't you think."

"You really should start calling her Mrs. Harker."

"Why?"

"Because my boyfriend would call her Mrs. Harker. Only her priest would call her Eva."

"And I'm not her priest anymore."

"No, you're not. And you don't want to keep reminding her that you used to be. It won't go well."

"Okay, Mrs. Harker it is. But it went well, didn't it?"

"She didn't stab you with a fork."

"I don't know why you say things like that. She's always seemed like a nice old lady to me."

"You've never pissed her off before," I pointed out.

"I think she's sweet. And I think you do, too."

When everything was heated up, Joseph and I pulled the little table over to the living area and we ate delicious leftovers while we watched Barbara Stanwyck tell lie after lie. And then, by the time she and the guy were finally falling for each other, Ross was getting sleepy. Brian noticed and said, "We should get going."

"But, the movie's not over," Franklin said—apparently his misgivings about the chauvinistic plot had evaporated.

"She gets the guy," I said.

"I know that, but how?"

"Hopefully by telling the truth," I said.

He turned to Brian and said, "We can leave at the next commercial. Maybe we can get home before it starts again." They were just around the corner, so it wasn't too unreasonable.

Brian rolled his eyes and nudged Ross. "Hey guy, you're coming with us."

"I am?"

"Don't you dare turn that into a dirty joke," Brian instructed.

The next commercial began and Franklin hustled them into their coats and winter boots. In a few minutes they were all gone and we were left with a room full of dirty dishes and a movie we'd hardly paid attention to. I started to pick up the dishes and Joseph told me to stop.

"I'll get up a half an hour early tomorrow and do

them then."

"Are you sure?"

"Worst case scenario, I'll go in a little late."

"Are you in a hurry to get to bed?" I asked.

"Absolutely." He kissed me and led me to the bedroom. Sitting down on the bed, he reached into the carved wooden box on the orange crate and pulled out a condom. He held it up and said, "It's time to get over this. You're going to put this on and you're going to fuck me."

"You're such a romantic."

"Shut up."

He stood up and began undressing me. In a matter of seconds he had me stripped naked. Which would have been far less impressive if I hadn't been tugging his clothes off at the same time. As I pulled down his tighty-whities, his cock jumped up hard and red, itching for a fight. I glanced at his face and caught him watching me. He gave me a little smile, just enough of a smile that his broken tooth showed. I loved that stupid tooth, and lived in terror that he might have it fixed.

There was no way out of this, I thought. I was going to have to fuck him. And I wanted to. I did. I missed fucking him. Missed thinking that safe sex made things truly safe. Missed thinking we had some control over our lives that it wasn't all just random.

He must have noticed that I was getting caught up in my thoughts because he said, "Nick?"

"What?"

"Suck me."

So, I did. I sucked him. He straddled me and reached behind himself to jack me off. Rolling his hips, he pulled his cock far enough out of my mouth that his ass was flirting with my prick. He moaned and pumped my mouth. Grabbing me by the hair.

Then he stopped. He got off me, picked up the condom and opened it. Then he rolled it down on my hard cock. He was about to spread K-Y all over it when I stopped him.

"Get another condom," I told him.

"Is this one not okay?"

"I want two."

"Oh Nick. You won't be able to feel anything."

"Just do it."

He reached into the box and pulled out another condom. He opened it and rolled it onto me. Then he grabbed the KY again, squeezed some onto his palm, and spread it all over my well-covered dick. He reached around and lubed himself up. Then he straddled me again, this time lowering himself onto my cock.

He was right. I couldn't feel a whole lot, some squeezing, but it didn't matter. The look on his face with me inside him was plenty. As he rode me, I lifted my hips to meet him. His mouth fell open in surprise when I did. He gasped and moaned and rode me harder. Reaching for the KY again, he squirted some onto his hand. He began jerking himself as I rested my hands on his thighs pushing him down on me over and over.

Then I flipped him over, reaching under him, grabbing him by the ass, holding him in just right so I could slam into him, hitting the right spot over and over. And it was the right spot, because I saw him lose control. His stomach tightened, squeezed, his fist pounded up and down on his own dick. His legs squeezed together, wrapping around me like a vise as he came, his cum flying onto both our stomachs. And then there was nothing; nothing but Joseph's eyes, half-closed and pale green in the dim bedroom light.

"Happy?" he asked.

And I was.

Chapter Seventeen

———————————————

I WAS up nearly two hours before sunrise. My mind buzzed with everything I needed to do. I snuck around and took a shower. Afterward, I very quietly dressed in jeans and a dark blue, thermal T-shirt. Then I slipped into the shoulder holster and took the black Cheetah down from the closet shelf where I'd been keeping it since I bought it in Vegas.

"Where are you going?" Joseph whispered.

"I had some ideas in the night. I have to check them out."

"Ideas that need a gun?"

"Possibly." I decided not to elaborate on that. "Can you call in sick and take Mrs. Harker to get her mammogram?"

"Oh, God, really? She won't like that." That was probably an understatement.

"I really need you to do that for me. I'll leave you the car. It's on Aldine on the other side of Broadway. I've written down Mrs. Harker's address," I set a slip of paper on the orange crate next to the bed. "She needs to be at Illinois Masonic by ten. Try to get her to take one of these." I set the prescription of Valium next to her address. "I call them easy pills. I've gotten her to take them before."

"Can I take one?"

"Only if you want to take a cab back and forth to Edison Park," I said, a little too sternly.

"I'm kidding."

"Sorry."

"Nick, be careful."

"I will be."

"No. You say that and then bad things happen. This time be careful."

I climbed onto the bed and kissed him. He smelled of sleep and peppermint and sage. I hugged him tight and promised, as sincerely as I could, that I'd be careful. I'm not sure I even convinced myself. Quickly, I slipped out of the apartment, closing the front door as quietly as I could so as not to wake Ross. Forgetting, of course, that he wasn't there.

I walked down to Aldine and took it across Boystown to my office on Clark. Once there, I grabbed the envelope I'd put together for the state's attorney. I wasn't entirely sure I was ready to take it to them, but it was good to have that option. And the last thing I could afford to do was spend time coming back to my office to get it.

Flipping the switch on my answering machine, I listened to my one message. It was Gloria Silver wishing me a Merry Christmas and asking if I'd had time to consider her offer. If she didn't knock it off soon, I was going to have to record her offering me money to kill someone and then turn it over to the cops.

Making an effort not to think about Gloria, I left and walked over to the El. I caught the Ravenswood and took it down to Merchandise Mart. I walked across the river at Wells. It was kind of awesome. Snow flurries filled the air and the sun was starting to rise. It was actually pretty gorgeous and I wished I could stand there on the bridge to appreciate it. At Wacker I turned right and walked down a block.

333 Wacker was a brand-new, curved building made of gorgeous teal-colored glass that reflected the river and the rising sun. It had opened about a year before. The lobby of 333 Wacker was done in green marble, gleaming silver chrome and black onyx accents. I came through the revolving doors and did what I usually do, looked like I belonged. There was a security guard standing around, but I quickly picked out the elevator bank that went to floors 14-24 and made a beeline. The fact that I was carrying a large manila envelope helped me blend in.

Most people in the Loop worked eight-thirty to five. Some worked earlier though, mailrooms in particular. I wanted the mailroom that was servicing Rita's office. I had some questions to ask. Still, I was far from alone in the lobby. There were a few people heading in the same direction. Women wearing big, puffy down coats and plastic boots, men wearing overcoats and galoshes or, those like me, willfully ruining a good pair of shoes.

In the elevator I hit 14. I would have liked to wander around the lobby and find the building's directory, but that would have drawn attention. The address for Lindquist Investigations was Suite 1423. The address for Rochelle LaRue was Suite 1583. My guess was that was somewhere near the mailroom.

The elevator door opened on fourteen. I eased my way past an executive or two and got out. Just to my right was a set of wooden double doors. In brass letters was the agency's name: Carney, Greenbaum and Turner, Attorneys at Law. I tried the doors but they were still locked.

I suspected someone was in, already working. Digging around in a pocket, I found my old Timex and saw that it was almost seven thirty. Yeah, someone was here already. I glanced down the hallway to my right and then the one to my left. It was a very typical, sparse office building hallway. Cream-colored with a bland brown carpet. There were doors at each end and several others along the way. I flipped a mental coin and went left. As I walked, I tried the doors. Locked. Locked. Locked. The one at the very end was open, though. I went in.

I was at the back of the building, which was flat. I passed several offices, the first of which was marked 1478. The next was 1476. I had a long way to go. As I walked, I noted that the view from the offices I was passing was not particularly good. These were the low-rent lawyers and paralegals. I reached the end of that hallway and had to make a sharp left. Now I was in a long, curved hallway and the view from the offices I was passing got a lot better. A couple were occupied, ambitious lawyers in early after the holiday. I kept my eyes front and pretended I knew where I was going. If anyone stopped me, I'd just ask for Rita.

I walked the entire curve, realizing as I did that this was one of the largest law firms I'd been in. Not that I'd been in a lot. It just never occurred to me that they could be this big. At about the middle of the curve, there was a large reception area that included a staircase to the fifteenth floor. I figured I'd come back to that in a few minutes.

Making it the rest of the way down the curve, I had to make another left. The numbers were getting a bit more to my liking. 1432, 1430. Fifty more feet and I was standing in front of Rita's office: 1423. It was an inner office. She didn't have a view. I wondered if that bothered her.

Like most of the other offices, her door stood open. That meant a couple of things. First, there wasn't anything valuable in her office. And second, she didn't want to make anyone at Carney, Greenbaum and Turner suspicious by keeping her door locked.

I walked in, figuring I'd take a look anyway. There was a small black desk, a chrome-and-black leather desk chair and a potted plant in the corner. The desk was clean; not a scrap of paper on it. Next to the phone was a small, framed photograph of Bill Appleton and Rita Lindquist. I grabbed it and quickly took the photo out of the frame, pushing it into my pocket. It might come in handy.

Walking around the desk, I sat in her chair. It was a little awkward since it was way too low. I felt like I was sitting on the floor. I didn't bother to adjust it since I knew I wouldn't be there long. I opened all the drawers and looked into them.

In one of the lower drawers were copies of every background check she'd done for Peterson-Palmer. They were filed and labeled with name and date. She'd organized them in date order. Bill Appleton was the fourth name. A quick glance let me know she'd rejected two of the three applicants before him. I suspected she'd done that to help him get the job. Not that it mattered.

In the other lower drawer were files for the cases she was working on for Carney, Greenbaum and Turner. Above that drawer were two more drawers. The middle drawer held her personalized stationary, LINDQUIST INVESTIGATIONS. *I really should get something like that,* I thought. The drawer above it held erasers, pencils, pens, an extra font ball for the IBM Selectric that sat on a metal cart shoved up against the wall. I wouldn't mind an IBM Selectric either.

Something snagged me and I went back to the middle drawer. I lifted up her stationary and underneath was another manila folder. This one said Gloria Silver on the tab. I didn't have time to look at it; instead, I started looking around the office. It really was very spare and neat in a pathological way.

I closed the door to look behind it and there on a hook was a green Marshall Field's bag. I took it off the hook and set the empty bag on the desk. I filled it with the manila envelope I'd brought and the Gloria Silver file. I decided against taking the Peterson-Palmer files. They had all of that and we didn't need her copies. I did grab everything she was working on for Carney, Greenbaum and Turner. That was grossly illegal, but then everything I'd done since I'd stepped into her office was illegal.

Leaving Rita's office, I made my way back to the reception area and the stairs to the fifteenth floor. As soon as I climbed the stairs I realized that Carney, Greenbaum and Turner was only renting half the fifteenth floor. There was another small reception area and double doors like the ones I'd encountered downstairs. I was only able to go to my right, though.

I followed the curve, passing a dozen nice offices, most of which were empty. Despite the lovely view, these offices would be less appealing since, presumably, they were away from the action downstairs. At that point, I made a sharp left.

Along this side of the floor were a dozen cubicles, each with its own word-processing computer. This was where the fine print was typed up over and over again. The hallway came to an abrupt end. To my left was a large copy room. To my right, the mailroom.

The mailroom was a large, square room with a big island in the center. There were counters and cabinets lining the walls. It was hard to say what it was all for, since the basic idea was mail came in and was immediately distributed.

There were three men sorting the mail. Well, there was one man of about forty sorting the mail. The other two were boys in their twenties, clearly just out of college, here temporarily while they applied to law schools.

They all looked up at me. For a moment, I wasn't sure what I was going to do. If I told the truth I'd get kicked out and then everything I had planned would be ruined. Then I got what I thought was a bright idea.

"I have a package for Rochelle LaRue."

The older guy, the one who worked, said, "Who?"

Meanwhile, one of the boys stepped forward and said, "I can take it."

"Can you step into the hallway for a moment?" I walked back out into the hallway.

A moment later, he came out to join me. He was a nice-looking kid who was carefully groomed and dressed for success. He wore a nice pair of slacks that probably had a matching jacket somewhere, a laundered white shirt and a red silk tie. His shoes were recently shined.

I didn't have a lot of time, and something about him pissed me off. Setting my Field's bag on the floor next to me, I turned around and slammed him up against the wall. Then I grabbed him by the neck and lifted. He was grimacing and standing on his tippy-toes.

"Rita Lindquist killed a friend of mine, so you're going to answer all of my questions without a problem. Do you understand?"

His eyes were wide as he struggled to nod his head. I eased off but kept my hand on his throat. He was shaking.

"She told you to collect any mail for Rochelle LaRue. What other names did she give you?"

He licked his lips. She had something on him and he didn't want to tell me the names. I squeezed a little tighter and said, "Don't make me break your neck."

That was a little more immediate than anything Rita knew about him. He started talking.

"Um, shit. Uh, Randi Lingstrom. That's Randi with an I. Walter Seyd. S-E-Y-D. Martin Goewy. G-O-E-W-Y."

"Is that it?"

"Yeah."

"What kind of mail did you get for them?"

"I dunno."

"No, you *do* know. You looked at the return addresses. You're that type."

"Official stuff. From the secretary of state. Records. Financial statements. Stuff like that."

"Financial statements from where?"

"Peterson-Palmer."

I let him go and stepped back. I looked down and noticed that there was a dark stain on his crotch and running down one pant leg. "Sorry about that," I said, then picked up my bag and walked away.

Chapter Eighteen

WHEN I LEFT 333 WACKER, I took a cab down to the financial district and Peterson-Palmer. It was nearly eight-thirty when I got there. I took the elevator to the twenty-second floor and found conference room A for a second time. I didn't bother going in. What I needed was the MIS department and Raymond Dewkes.

For the second time that morning, I found myself wandering around an office space, trying doors and snooping down hallways. This building had a very different feel. For one thing, it was older and the furnishings were far from trendy. For another, the building was square—unlike 333 Wacker, whose floor plan probably looked something like the chopped off top of an ice cream cone.

I found an unlocked door near the men's room and wandered around looking for Raymond. I didn't find him right away. Instead I found a glass room with two rows of mainframe computers that looked like closet-sized, reel-to-reel tape players. That made me think Raymond had to be nearby.

Walking along the outer edge of the building, I looked

into each office. Most were still empty. Some people would be showing up a few minutes late the day after a holiday. A lot of people would have taken Wednesday through Friday as vacation days. I picked up a few puzzled looked from the few people I did run across.

Finally, I came to Raymond's office. He sat behind his desk staring at a cup of coffee and a muffin as though they might be about to say something profound. He look up and saw me.

"Oh, you."

"You know that Vincent's dead, don't you?"

"Yeah, we found out on Monday. It's a real bummer."

"Do you know that Rita and Bill are the ones who killed him?"

His face fell. "What? No. You're shitting me."

"They poisoned him."

"Are they in jail?"

"No. The police haven't been able to prove anything yet. That's why I need your help."

"To prove they killed Vincent?"

"Not exactly. They stole a lot of money and I think they're going to try to get at it this morning."

He looked at me suspiciously and said, "Uh-huh."

"I need you too look up some accounts for me."

"The ones I got you before?"

"No, different ones."

He waved me in and said, "Close the door." He dug around in his pocket and took out a ring of keys. He slipped one into a lock on the left side of his computer and turned it. Then he powered up the computer.

"I just got here. Haven't even logged on." He noticed me looking suspiciously at the computer. "This is the new IBM AT, 16-bit processor, 512 K RAM, 20 MEG internal disk, 1.2 on a floppy."

Against the wall was a bookshelf that had a lot of thick books with IBM logos. This looked like it might be as challenging as the law. Possibly more.

"Everything you just said is a foreign language to me."

"It is a language. Several actually. Some of which are even called languages."

"Great."

He glanced at the computer. "This is the C prompt. Most of the people who work here just get the user-interface for the company. I'm one of the people who designed that, so I start out…kind of behind it, in case I need to tinker."

"Uh-huh." It sounded like he was saying he was the man behind the curtain. Like the Great and Powerful Oz. It also sounded like he was dumbing things down for me.

He typed in a few words and the screen changed. Amber symbols on a dark background spelled out PETERSON-PALMER. At the bottom of the screen was an empty box. Raymond typed something into the box and the screen changed.

"This is the basic navigation screen. Who do you want to look at?"

"Uh, Randi, with an I, Lingstrom."

He typed that in and the screen changed again. "Okay, that's a little weird."

"What is?"

"Everything she has is cash. Most of our clients own things: mutual funds, bonds, stocks. Her money's just sitting there, not earning money."

"How much does she have?"

"Four hundred, thirty-seven thousand, five hundred and fifty."

"Was it recently converted to cash?"

A few more clicks. "Last Wednesday."

"Look up Martin Goewy. G-O-E-W-Y."

Raymond hit a couple of keys and we were back at the lookup screen. Then he input Martin Goewy.

"No, nothing."

"Walter Seyd. S-E-Y-D."

He typed again. The screen changed.

"Okay, yeah, he's got more than three hundred thousand. Also in cash. What's going on?"

"Those are accounts that Appleton set up for Rita and himself. They have fake identities to go with those names. What I need you to tell me is how will they get that money."

"We could write them a check. That would probably take a couple of days. They could wire the money somewhere. That would be faster."

"But they'd actually have to physically come in here, right?"

"Not necessarily. We have branch offices."

"Can you do anything to prevent them from accessing the money?"

"I can freeze the accounts. But... I mean, I could get fired for that."

"This is money they stole from Peterson-Palmer clients. And don't forget, they killed Vincent. They want the money to get away."

Raymond was still nervous about it, but he hit a few keys and then went back to the previous record and hit a few keys there. I took the Timex out of my pocket and glanced at it. It was two minutes after nine.

"The branch offices open at nine," he said.

"How many are there?"

"Just five: Skokie, Park Ridge, Evanston, Naperville and Winnetka."

"Will you be able to tell if someone tries to get into those accounts?"

"Yeah, but it's not easy. We do a nightly run to look at that sort of thing."

My mind was racing, trying to grasp things I didn't know much about. Then something hit me. "Wait, wait, do we really need to stop them? I mean, if they move the money we'll know where it went, right? We'll be able to trace them wherever they go."

"Yes and no," Raymond said.

"What does that mean?"

"Working here you kind of pick up things."

That didn't sound good. "Okay."

"They're probably going to wire the money offshore. Probably to the Caribbean."

"And you can't trace it after that?"

"You can. You just need a court order and lawyers, and that all takes a couple of weeks. In the meantime, they'll wire the money back to the United States. They'll split it up into a half a dozen accounts, then take out cash, as much as the bank will allow, from each account. That money goes into a clean account somewhere that we can't trace."

"They're laundering the money," I said. "Okay, so we do have to stop them. They're at the branch office and they can't get into their accounts. What happens then?"

"Um, well, the agent will probably call the Help Desk."

"Is the Help Desk able to see that you've locked their accounts?"

"Yes, but I don't think they know they can."

"Aren't they supposed to know things like that?"

"Mostly they help people reboot their computers after a crash, or someone can't figure out how to sign on or do basic input. They kick all the sophisticated issues up to me."

"So, you'll get a call and you can ask which branch they're at."

"Yes."

"Then we just need to figure out how to keep—"

There was a knock on the door.

"Help desk?" I asked.

"They usually call."

I opened the door and found two people standing there. One was a rumpled looking man of about forty, wearing slacks, a white shirt and a loosened tie. He looked like he'd already worked a twelve-hour day. The other was a youngish woman in a crisp, black business suit with a frilly lavender blouse underneath. I noticed Raymond sit up straighter in this chair. This wasn't necessarily good.

"Raymond, we got a call from an agent out in Naperville. Did you block two accounts this morning?" the man asked. I assumed he was Raymond's boss.

"Hello, I'm Nick Nowak. I'm contracted to do security for Peterson-Palmer." Well, it was kind of true. "And you are?"

"Jim Tinker, director, MIS."

I glanced at the young woman.

"Jill Smith, vice president, Human Resources," she said, timidly. She was clearly anxious.

"You were Vincent Renaldi's boss?" I asked her.

"Yes. I'm confused, who are you?"

"Nick Nowak. Vincent hired me."

"To work for Rita?"

"No. To investigate Rita Lindquist and Bill Appleton."

"What's going on?" Tinker asked, then glared at Raymond. "Did you lock those accounts on his authority?"

"The accounts belong to Rita and Bill."

"No, they don't," Tinker said. "Those aren't the names—"

"I need to sit down," Jill said, as she stumbled into Raymond's ancient, guest chair.

"Okay, how did the two of you get here? Who called who?"

"Wait, I have no idea who you are or why you think you're in—"

"Rita called me," Jill said. "She said the accounts were locked and I needed to come down here and find out what was happening with them."

"And why are you doing it?" I asked.

"She…my daughter is in preschool. She mentioned the name of the preschool and where it is. She implied—"

"She threatened your daughter?"

Jill nodded. It might not be the whole story, but it was enough for now. I needed Rita and Bill to sit tight in Naperville. But I wasn't entirely sure how to do that.

"Does your system ever go down?" Joseph talked about how their system at FirstChicago went down all the time. My guess was it happened everywhere.

"Rarely." Tinker said.

"Yes, all the time," Jill said.

"Can you make it go down?" I asked.

"Yes, but we're not going to. Trades are being made, people are working."

"Can you take down just Naperville?"

"No, not individually, we'd have to take down all the satellite offices."

"Do it," Jill said.

"You can't authorize that," Tinker told her.

She pulled her self together and stood up. "I'm going to get my daughter. I'll call Mr. Palmer from my car." Giving Raymond a very intense look she added, "Don't unlock those accounts unless you get the say so from Mr. Palmer, do you understand?"

"You can't just give instructions to people who report to me," Tinker sputtered.

"Fine. You explain to Mr. Palmer why these criminals escaped with our client's money."

He turned to Raymond and said, "Don't unlock the accounts unless *I* tell you to."

"Miss Smith, before you leave. I need you to call Rita back and tell her that the company is having computer problems and you've been told they'll be back up at, um, noon." I hoped that would give me enough time.

"Do I have to do that?" she asked.

"Yes."

She took a deep breath and picked up Raymond's phone. After dialing a few numbers she stood there biting her lip. "Yes, can you put Edward on?" More lip biting. "Edward, you're with two clients? A man and a woman, right?" She listened to his answer. "Can you put the woman on?"

A moment later she said, "Rita…" She shivered a little as she said it. "I just went up to the MIS department. Apparently there's a glitch and all the offices will be down until noon."

She listened for a moment.

"If you let me know where to reach you, I can call you the minute the system is back up."

She listened again.

"I have no idea. Honestly, I don't know a lot about computers to begin—Rita you don't have to threaten me. I've done what you asked. I went up to MIS and found out what was happening. Now you just need to be patient while they fix the problem. Just go have coffee somewhere. We'll have this fixed before you know it."

The poor woman was pale and a sweat had broken out on her upper lip, but her voice stayed calm and reasonable.

Chapter Nineteen

THE FIRST THING I did was the right thing to do. It didn't work out, but it was the right thing. I called Town Hall and asked for Detective Gardner, only to be told he was taking an extra day for the holiday. I asked for whoever was handling his cases. A Detective Waddington came to the phone. I didn't know him and he didn't know me, but he was still nice enough to tell me that both Vincent's murder and the Ponzi scheme it was meant to cover up had been turned over to the county sheriff's Financial Crimes Unit. I called the sheriff's office and, after being transferred three or four times, learned that the case had not yet been assigned. Vincent's murder had been left in a bureaucratic crack while his killers skipped town. That left me with one choice. The wrong choice.

I needed a car. Raymond didn't have one, but he did call their travel person for me and found out there was a Hertz office a few blocks away—and I could use the Peterson-Palmer discount. He gave me the address of the Naperville office and wished me luck.

The Hertz office was at Washington and Wells, attached to a self-park garage. It was only big enough for a one-person sales counter and a giant poster of O.J. Simpson running to catch a plane. The clerk—a very bored black girl of around twenty-one—set me up with a white Ford Escort. I took it as a personal commentary.

Once I'd signed the paperwork, she gave me the keys, told me the car was on the seventh floor of the self-park, and gave me a validated ticket so I could leave the garage without emptying my bank account. Before I left the rental office, I bought a map of Illinois. I'd been to Naperville once, to see Gloria, a few years back. That didn't mean I knew where I was going.

When I got to the seventh floor of the garage, there were five white Escorts in close proximity. I'd thrown the rental agreement into the Field's bag, so I had to retrieve it and look for the license number. I figured out which Escort was mine and walked over. The car was a coupe with a notched hatchback. It was kind of perky and looked like a wonderful gift for a cheerleader on her seventeenth birthday. A very short cheerleader.

I opened the driver's door, tossed the Field's bag onto the passenger seat, and immediately positioned the seat so that it was all the way back. I climbed in and adjusted the seat back so it lay at an angle. It was uncomfortable and cramped, but I'd driven worse.

Feeling like I should get my bearings before I left, I opened up the map and reached into my pocket for my cigarettes. The pocket was empty, of course. I was now a nonsmoker. I spent a moment regretting that decision yet again, then forced myself to focus on the map. I was going to take the Eisenhower out to Route 88 and eventually find a thoroughfare to take me to downtown Naperville and a tiny little segment of Chicago Avenue.

I drove down seven ramps and gave the attendant my validated ticket. Then I turned south on Wells—my only

choice—and went down about ten blocks until I got to
Congress. After taking a quick right, I landed almost immediately on the Eisenhower, dipping underneath the gigantic
main post office. I expected it to take me at least an hour to
get to Naperville. That would put me in front of the Peterson-Palmer office around eleven. It also gave me time to
come up with a plan.

Since I'd failed to interest any law enforcement agency in
Rita and Bill, I had to think up a way to stop them, or at
least slow them down. The only thing I could think of was
walking into the Peterson-Palmer office after they returned,
and explaining that they wouldn't be getting their money and
that I knew their fake names.

Now, they might have other fake names, though I
suspected three identities was all Rita thought she'd ever
need. I mean, seriously, it's hard to imagine her thinking,
"Wait, I might need a fourth identity." That said, she might
have a fourth identity prepared or she might be able to put a
new one together on short notice. She was clearly good at
creating new selves.

They also might have other bank accounts. Not all the
money was accounted for in the Peterson-Palmer accounts.
They wanted to wire the money somewhere, which meant
there was definitely at least one offshore account. And the
corporations they'd created all had bank accounts. There
might be money there—of course, Rita had abandoned
Rochelle LaRue, leaving her identification at the condo. So
she couldn't get at that money. On top of that, my guess was
those accounts were pretty scant.

No, I figured there were other accounts, but whose
names they were under I had no idea. Looking at Rita and
Bill was like looking at an iceberg. Was I looking at the
iceberg or was I looking at the tip?

I wasn't even all the way to Oak Park before I became

concerned that I might chew my arm off so I didn't have to think about how much I wanted a cigarette. I had a feeling it was going to be a long time before that urge went away. I should have bought Joseph a bathrobe that day at Field's. It really wasn't a bad idea. He would have looked cute in a terry cloth robe. And I could be smoking a Marlboro as I merged onto Route 88.

As much as I wanted to see the look on their faces when they realized they'd never get their hands on their money and their identities were blown, I knew the best idea was keeping a low profile, waiting for them to give up on the idea of getting the money, and following them back to wherever they were holed up. Once I knew where they were staying, I could go home, wait until tomorrow morning, and call the sheriff's office to find out who was handling the case.

I got off the freeway at Naperville Road. The first thing I did was start looking for a convenience store where I could buy some gum. Unfortunately, there was nothing but dead grass, crunchy old piles of dirty snow and sprawling office buildings.

It was starting to rain, so I looked around the Escort's dashboard and found the windshield wipers. I started passing more businesses—a Mickey D's, a Mobil station, a branch of Midtown Bank—but none that sold gum. Then I was back in an undeveloped area of mainly trees. I christened it the Naperville National Forest. There were occasional houses and walled off developments, but basically it was trees and dirty snow until I reached a big intersection. One of the streets was Chicago Avenue, so I turned onto it figuring I'd eventually find downtown Naperville that way.

Almost immediately, I noticed a well-manicured strip mall with a 7-Eleven. I pulled in, parked, and went into the store. Ten minutes later, I walked out with six packs of Wrigley gum: two each of Spearmint, Juicy Fruit and

Doublemint; two E.T. heads filled with gum—they were probably stale but I couldn't resist; three chocolate bars; some Starbursts; and a bag of potato chips. I was going to need something to do while I sat in front of Peterson-Palmer and these were all better options that chewing off my arm.

I squeezed back into the rental, shoved two pieces of Juicy Fruit into my mouth, and got back on Chicago Avenue. Ten minutes later I'd found downtown Naperville. The portion of Chicago Avenue that included the Peterson-Palmer office looked like something out of an old Jimmy Stewart movie, the kind that ends happily and even the bad guys turn out not to be so bad in the end. It had a lot of old, two-story brick buildings from the 1890s. I swear one of them was a soda fountain.

The Peterson-Palmer office was in a restored brick building. The front door was glass, brass and highly varnished wood. There were two plate glass windows, one on each side of the door. The window on the right boasted the very austere Peterson-Palmer logo, while the other window had nothing but a few streaks from the rain that was falling.

Through each window, I could see a financial advisor waiting to talk to a client. All in all, it looked like a lovely place to go and discuss how wealthy you were and how much more wealthy you were going to become.

I picked a spot west of the building about half a block away. There were trees and cars and people around, so it was as far away as I could get and still be able to see who was going into the entrance of the building.

I settled in for a long wait. There was a little nook in the dashboard left of the steering wheel next to the speedometer. I started piling up my candy there for later. I rolled down the window, spit out my gum, and then promptly ate the bag of chips. I crumpled up the empty bag and threw it into the back seat. Then I pulled Rita's files out of the Field's bag and started looking through them.

First, I put Gloria's file back into the bag. I knew that would have some interesting tidbits in it, so I decided to look at it later when I had more time. First, I wanted to see what Rita was up to at Carney, Greenbaum and Turner. I wasn't sure what kind of law they specialized in. My morning walk around their offices told me they were a very large firm, and that they made a lot of money, which probably meant they had several specialties.

I flipped through the files I'd taken—well, stolen—and noticed right off that most of them were The People of Illinois v. So-and-So. What that normally meant was criminal. Glancing through the first few files, I picked up pretty quickly on the firm's specialty: rich people. Rich people who punched their neighbors in the face, drove home after thirteen or fourteen cocktails, or were still totally convinced that cocaine was not addictive.

About half way through the stack, I found a file called People of Illinois v DeCarlo. That was the case Terry was involved with. Well, more accurately, that was the case we were trying to keep Terry out of. We didn't want him testifying, didn't think he'd do well on the stand. Oh shit—Rochelle LaRue. The name was familiar not because it sounded like a drag queen, though it still did, but because that was the name Rita used when she pretended to be a social worker and did her best to intimidate Terry.

I wondered if that was Rita's specialty, witness intimid—

The passenger window shattered. A woman's hand reached in, pulled up the lock, and opened the door. Meanwhile, I shoved the Field's bag into the back seat and reached into my coat for my Chettah. Moments later it was muzzle to muzzle with Rita's .38 Special.

"NICK NOWAK," Rita said, making herself comfortable in the passenger seat. The thick fur coat she wore protected her from any glass that had fallen on to the seat.

"Rita Lindquist."

"I feel like I know you."

"I feel like I don't want to know you."

"I'm guessing you had something to do with our accounts being shut down."

"Bingo."

"That little faggot in MIS did it, didn't he?"

"Which little faggot? I can never keep track."

"The one Vincent fucked in Conference Room A last Thursday morning."

"You have a vivid imagination." I was bluffing, of course. I was fairly certain that had actually happened.

"No, I have a voice-activated recording device in each of the conference rooms at Peterson-Palmer."

I really did need to learn more about bugs and listening devices and all that. Not so I could start doing it—it was very illegal—but so I'd remember to look around and see if someone else was doing it.

"Is that why you killed Vincent? Because he fucked little Raymond."

"No. I killed him because you were getting too close and I didn't want him getting you anymore information."

"And you didn't kill my friends because you wanted me distracted."

"I wanted you dead. I just didn't realize you were running a boarding house and would share all the cookies."

"We have guests. People do that over the holidays."

"I know what people do. I've spent enough time watching them."

"So, how are we going to do this, Rita? Are we going to kill each other in downtown Naperville?"

"Look behind you."

That didn't sound good. I looked over my shoulder and there was Bill Appleton hunched over outside the Escort holding his own .38 Special. Aimed directly at me.

"Give me your gun," Rita demanded.

"Well, look at the two of you. Bonnie and Clyde," I said. I really didn't know what I wanted to do next. Giving them my gun seemed like a really bad idea; not giving it to them also seemed like a really bad idea.

"What do you think you're going to do with me?"

"Trade you. For our money."

I burst out laughing.

"Why do you think that's funny?"

"Because it is funny. You killed the only person at Peterson-Palmer who might have cared enough about me to release the money. Most of the people there don't know me from Adam. They'll probably think I'm part of your plot."

"Fine. Come up with a better idea."

"Why would I do that?"

"Because we have two guns aimed at you."

"If your boyfriend shoots me in the back of the head it's going to make a lot of noise on a quiet, well populated street in a suburb that prides itself on its low crime rate." I was really just guessing on the last part, but it seemed plausible. "You might as well call him off. If he shoots me everything's over. The two of you go to jail and somehow I don't think that's your goal."

She caught Bill's eye and nodded her head in a way that told him to back off. "What if I shoot you? It wouldn't be as loud."

"Except for the window you broke."

"I'm starting not to care."

"I do still have a gun. If you shoot me, I shoot you. I think you care about that."

"I want my money. It was hard to earn."

"Stealing isn't as easy as people think, is it?"

"Stop being a smart ass and help me get my money."

"It's not going to happen. By now Mr. Palmer knows everything you did and those accounts are locked and you're never going to open them."

Appleton had come around the car and was standing behind Rita. "What's going on? Are we gonna get the money soon?"

"He says they've locked the accounts and there's no way to open them."

"Well, that's his fault, isn't it? He made them do that. He told them about the accounts. He told them to lock the accounts. We need to get out of here, Rita. We need to put an end—"

And that's when he raised his gun, holding it over her shoulder as if he were going to shoot me. So I shot him first. He crumpled to the ground while Rita screamed. Whether she was mad that I'd shot her boyfriend or she thought I was trying to shoot her, I don't know. What I do know is she squeezed off a shot at me and then climbed out of the car, stumbled over her boyfriend and ran away.

I wasn't even sure she'd hit me until I began to feel woozy and the world went black, like a TV show abruptly ending.

Chapter Twenty

WHOEVER SAID that what doesn't kill you makes you stronger is someone I'd like to find and pummel with a steel rod. Whatever doesn't kill you leaves a nasty scar you have to live with forever. I'm not a fan of scars. They're unsightly and they hurt.

When you have a flesh wound in the movies you get up off the floor and chase the bad guys until you catch them. In real life, the bullet shatters a rib, nicks one lung and does a real number on your shoulder blade. You end up having a three-hour long emergency surgery and an invitation to come back to do it all again in six months.

I can't honestly say I remember much about the three days after I was shot. Between the surgery, recovering from the surgery, and being given a handful of Darvon every few hours so I didn't feel the pain from the gunshot wound, I spent a lot of those three days out cold. It was Friday by the time I started to think clearly. That afternoon, Joseph came by with Mrs. Harker. She sat in the guest chair next to my bed looking subdued. He stood by the bed looking down at me.

"Where am I?" I asked.

"County."

"How did that happen?"

"They took you to an E.R. in Aurora, I think. Made sure you were stable and brought you down here. They have more experience with gunshot wounds. The doctor who did your surgery is supposed to be quite good."

"And they're being good? Telling you stuff?" Hospitals didn't always want to give your boyfriend information.

"No. But they'll tell your mother."

"My mother?"

I had the horrible thought that my family was lurking outside my room. Instead, though, Mrs. Harker said, "I tell lies."

"And we've been going to confession every morning so that she's instantly absolved." They seemed to be working things through, which was good since the drugs didn't really let me think about them long enough to—

"What happened to Bill Appleton? Did I kill him?"

"No. He wasn't badly hurt."

"Is he in jail?"

"Yes."

"And Rita?"

"She's still missing."

I tried to absorb that. She was gone. They were unlikely to find her. But it was also true that she wasn't off living the life of leisure she'd planned, so I might have accomplished something. Or maybe I'd just sent her out into the world to rob and maim and kill a whole new bunch of people. Shit.

"Can you help me sit up?"

We adjusted the bed. Then Joseph helped me slide into a more comfortable position. There were curtains all around my bed, so I couldn't tell how many other people were in the room with me. My guess was at least three. A TV was playing nearby and someone was moaning.

Then I noticed that Joseph was holding the Marshall Field's bag I'd had the day of the shooting.

"Where did you get that?" I asked.

"The police released the rental car yesterday, so Brian and I went out to Naperville and got it so we could turn it in. This was in the back seat."

"How much did the rental car cost?"

"Don't know yet. You got the insurance, but the window is going to be under the cost of the deductible. We don't know yet if the insurance will cover the costs of cleaning the car."

"What do you mean? Why do we have to clean it?"

"Nick, you bled everywhere. It was very unpleasant driving to the rental place."

"Oh. Sorry."

Then I remembered things we'd said before I went to Naperville. "I did try to be careful."

"I know. We talked about that yesterday."

"I don't remember yesterday."

"That's probably a good thing."

"So, what's today?"

"Friday."

"Something was supposed to happen today."

"Yeah." He turned and said, "Mrs. Harker, can we have a minute?"

She got up and came over to the bed and said, "You are stupid man."

"I know," I said, as I watched her leave the room. I looked up at Joseph and asked, "How are the two of you getting along?"

He scrunched his face up and said, "Priest is priest."

"Oh good. You're talking."

"We saw the doctor for her results. That's the thing that was happening today."

"Oh." The look on his face told me a lot. "Bad, huh?"

"Stage four ovarian cancer with a couple of small tumors in her right breast."

"Wow. She seems pretty okay."

"I'm not sure she understands. She asked if she'd have to have surgery and Dr. Macht said, 'No, it was too late for that.' I'm not sure she heard much after 'no.'"

"Since she's not having surgery, she thinks she's not that sick."

"Exactly."

"What about radiation?"

"At this point it would only make her worse."

"So she doesn't have to make any decisions?"

"Just how much pain medication she wants."

"I guess it's okay if she doesn't really understand, you know?"

"I suppose," he said, reluctantly.

"If she was twenty, facing this might be a lot more important. But at her age, I'm not sure it matters."

"You look tired. We should let you rest."

"But you came. You should stay."

"I'll take Mrs. Harker down to the cafeteria for lunch and then we'll come back. Do you want your bag?"

"Yeah, sure."

Days before I was looking at Rita's cases for Carney, Greenbaum and Turner. I wanted to continue. Joseph gave me the bag and then kissed me. "Be back soon."

I started leafing through the folders, wondering why the Naperville police hadn't taken them as evidence in the shooting, and then before I could even open the first file, drifted off to sleep.

Sometime later I woke up to find Jill Smith next to my

bed staring at me like I was an exhibit in a museum. She wore a full-length down coat and hadn't made any attempt to take it off.

"Oh, you're awake." She sounded sorry about that.

"Don't count on it. It doesn't last long."

"Mr. Palmer wanted me to come down and assure you that you have a job with us when you get out of here."

"Thank you."

"And we'll be picking up your medical expenses."

"Including the second surgery in six months?"

"Oh, um, I'll talk to Mr. Palmer about that."

"Thank you."

I had medical insurance, it just wasn't the kind that actually covered medical expenses. From my experience their main function was to cash my check every month. Unfortunately, it was what I could afford.

"We've been able to recover almost two-thirds of the money our clients lost."

"Did you get money from Gloria Silver?"

"Yes. She's been cooperative. Almost helpful."

Someone was trying to stay out of jail.

"Rita's still missing."

"Yes. But I'm sure she's thousands of miles away."

"Put your daughter in a different school. Use a fake name."

The poor woman turned so pale I thought she might faint.

————

SUGAR PILSON WAS GETTING married and I was desperate for a cigarette. I had gotten out of the hospital on the morning of New Year's Eve and spent most of the day in bed. Joseph and Brian had gone down to Carson Pirie Scott and bought me a double-breasted navy suit with wide lapels and gigantic shoulders. It was too big, but I think they'd done that on purpose so that it would be easier to get me in and out of it.

My right arm was in a sling so that I wouldn't move my shoulder blade around. I wore a nicely pressed white shirt, a brass collar bar that pushed the knot on my tie forward, a red-and-navy striped tie, and an over-sized, red silk scarf as my sling. I was still taking a lot of pain medication, so I put up very little resistance to Joseph and Brian dressing me up like a six-foot-three Ken doll.

The wedding was at Sugar's home at midnight. It was going to be small. No more than fifty people. Most of the furniture on the first floor had magically disappeared and white, wooden folding chairs had taken its place in the double living room. In the dining room, beneath the very large portrait of a flamingo that had brought the happy couple together, the table was covered with a delicious-looking buffet and a stack of wedding gifts. I hadn't bought her anything, but I suppose getting the skinny on her fiancé was a decent gift. I had no intention of sending her an invoice, after all.

At eleven thirty, there were waiters wandering around with champagne in flutes. Joseph snagged one going by.

"You can't have any," he said to me. "Do you want me to find you a pop?"

"Can I at least take an extra pain pill?"

"Dr. Macht said you should start trying to cut back."

"What does he know? Has he ever been shot?"

Joseph gave me a disapproving look and went off to find me a nonalcoholic beverage. The house began to fill up. At the front door, a pretty girl hung coats on a rented garment rack. People were still coming in a steady stream. I began to wonder if Sugar's idea of fifty people was actually a hundred.

Someone touched my right elbow and pain shot through me like an electric current. I turned and there was Gloria Silver. For a moment, I wished I'd brought my gun. She wore a purple cocktail dress with ruffles on both shoulders, sequins on the bodice and more ruffles around the hips. It was a very trendy dress and one that made no sense on her. Gloria was a woman who'd starved herself into a sleek angularity. This dress restored the curves she'd struggled to get rid of.

"You should have accepted my offer. If you were a little less scrupulous you might not have gotten shot."

I didn't really consider murder-for-hire to be "a little less scrupulous," but to each his own.

"You do know that even asking me to kill Rita for you is considered a crime."

"I can't tell if you really are a Goody Two-shoes or if it's just me you don't like."

"Is there a reason it can't be both?" I asked. "Come to think of it, Gloria, I'm a little surprised you're not in prison."

"Well, I do like to be surprising." Then she looked across the room and yelled, "Yvonne! Darling! You look divine!" As she crossed the room, I heard her saying, "Isn't this all just picture perfect."

It was picture perfect. A light snow was falling outside, the kind that wouldn't last long since it was warm, in the thirties. There was a harpist in the hallway plucking away. Everyone looked their best, a new year, a new marriage. It was perfect.

Joseph came back with Coca-Cola in a crystal glass. "I just saw Brian. You're wanted upstairs."

"Okay."

"Can you make it on your own?" Joseph asked.

"Of course I can make it on my own. I wasn't shot in the foot." The hovering was beginning to wear thin. It was nice to be pampered; it was terrible to need it. I walked back out to the foyer and stood at the bottom of the stairs. The bannister was on the right, meaning I'd have to walk up without holding onto anything. I would probably be fine, but if I lost my balance there was no way to steady myself. I handed the cola to the coat-check girl, then walked up, slowly, pushing each foot all the way onto the step. I made it in about twice the time it would usually take.

I followed the hallway down to Sugar's bedroom. I found her sitting on one of the sofas surrounded by Brian, her hair-dresser, her makeup artist, two maids of honor and a partridge in a pear tree. Really. There was a Christmas tree in the corner and it had a bird on top that I assumed was a partridge.

Sugar's dress was not something most women would wear to get married. It was short, simple and almost pink. It was sleeveless, satin and covered in a layer of matching lace. She wore three tennis bracelets on her left wrist, a pair of large diamond studs in her ears, a simple pendant with a single, dime-sized diamond around her neck and a cocktail ring on her right hand that was a giant pink sapphire surrounded by more diamonds. Her hair was swept up and there were tiny flowers in it. She was smoking a cigarette—something she rarely did—and, I wanted to snatch it out of her jewel-encrusted hand.

Seeing me, she said, "Darling, you're up and about."

She got up and took a step toward me. I said, "Careful."

"Air kisses only. I understand." She air-kissed me twice.

"What is Gloria Silver doing here?"

"It's been a busy week. We buried the hatchet."

"How much did the funeral cost?"

A twinkle in her eyes told me I'd hit that right on the nose. Putting out the cigarette, she came around the coffee table and led me over to the bedroom portion of the enormous room. We sat down on the bed and quietly, so as not to be heard across the room, she said, "I paid her back the money she'd given Michael for his house. And a tiny bit extra. Apparently, she desperately needs cash."

She could be reimbursing Peterson-Palmer for the Ponzi scheme. Or she could be gearing up to pay a team of lawyers to keep her out of jail. I wasn't sure which. I'd read the paper that morning and there wasn't anything in it about Rita and Bill.

Of course, if Gloria was smart she'd probably already gotten herself a good attorney and was negotiating a super secret plea deal. If she guided them through the scheme there might be enough paperwork on the pair to put them away without Gloria ever showing her face in court.

"Be careful of Gloria. I think she has something on you."

"Of course she has something on me. But I have more on her. She wasn't very discreet when she was with Michael."

That put a few points in his column. Still, I had to ask, "Is this really what you want, Sugar?"

"Michael? Yes, he is what I want. And thank you…I really prefer to go into these things with my eyes open and you made that possible."

"You aren't afraid he might try to cheat you?"

"Oh, I imagine he will. But I think they'll be small, little cheats here and there just to keep his hand in."

"And you can live with that?"

"Darling, you should know this already—there is no such thing as the perfect man. They're all broken. The trick is finding one who's broken in a way you like."

"And you like the way he's broken?"

"I do," she said, then giggled. "I said that too soon. I'm not supposed to say it until later."

Brian came over with a few last-minute details and I excused myself to go back downstairs. Going down was easier than coming up. I could put my left hand on the rail and I felt secure. The coat-check girl had put my pop on a side table. I took it back.

When I made it into the double living room, I saw that people were sitting down. *It must be nearing midnight,* I thought. I found Joseph; he'd taken a couple of seats on the left side near the front. I slid in next to him.

"Is everything okay?"

"Yes, I think everything is going to be fine."

I spotted Michael France hanging around in the hallway outside the far half of the living room. He was nervously pacing, though he looked happy enough. The harpist was joined by a flute player and the two of them began a lovely duet. It took me a moment or two before I recognized it as "Stairway to Heaven." I didn't remember the lyrics well, but I had the feeling that beyond the title it wasn't exactly a wedding song. And then we turned around and watched as Sugar came down the aisle. She was smiling. Michael was smiling. Brian. The minister who seemed to have arrived out of nowhere. Everyone was smiling. They were all happy. Maybe it was the pills I was taking, but I couldn't feel it. Their happiness felt gossamer thin.

The weight of the last few weeks suddenly bore down on me. Mrs. Harker's illness. The poisoning of my friends. Vincent Renaldi's death. Rita Lindquist's escape. Horrible things. Part of me wished I'd stayed home to lick my wounds. At that moment, I thought I'd prefer my bed to smiling as the New Year began. As though he'd read my thoughts, Joseph slid his hand into mine and squeezed.

"We can leave as soon as they're married," he whispered.

Life is pain. Life is danger. Life is love. There have been times when I have hidden from life. It didn't work. Life found me. Love found me. Try as I might, I could not hide.

"No," I whispered back. "Let's stay a while."

Also by Marshall Thornton

The Perils of Praline

Desert Run

Full Release

The Ghost Slept Over

My Favorite Uncle

Femme

Praline Goes to Washington

Night Drop: A Pinx Video Mystery

Hidden Treasures: A Pinx Video Mystery

IN THE BOYSTOWN MYSTERIES SERIES

Boystown: Three Nick Nowak Mysteries

Boystown 2: Three More Nick Nowak Mysteries

Boystown 3: Two Nick Nowak Novellas

Boystown 4: A Time For Secrets

Little Boy Dead

Boystown 5: Murder Book

Boystown 6: From The Ashes

Boystown 7: Bloodlines

Boystown 8: The Lies That Bind

Boystown 9: Lucky Days

Little Boy Afraid

About the Author

Marshall Thornton is the author of the popular *Boystown* series. He has been a finalist for the Lambda Award five times and won once. His romantic comedy, *Femme* is currently a Lambda finalist for Best Gay Romance. Other books include *My Favorite Uncle*, The *Ghost Slept Over* and *Desert Run*. He is a member of Mystery Writers of America.

CPSIA information can be obtained
at www.ICGtesting.com
Printed in the USA
LVOW03s0111120318
569503LV00001B/112/P